T0071777

JAMAICA KINCAID
SEE NOW THEN

Jamaica Kincaid was born in St. John's, Antigua. Her books include *At the Bottom of the River*, *Annie John*, *Lucy*, *The Autobiography of My Mother*, *My Brother*, and *Mr. Potter*, all published by FSG. She teaches at Harvard University.

SEE
NOW
THEN

SEE
NOW
THEN

JAMAICA
KINCAID

FARRAR, STRAUS AND GIROUX NEW YORK

Farrar, Straus and Giroux
18 West 18th Street, New York 10011

Published in 2013 by Farrar, Straus and Giroux
First paperback edition, 2014

The Library of Congress has cataloged the hardcover edition as follows:
Kincaid, Jamaica.
    See now then / Jamaica Kincaid. — 1st ed.
        p.   cm.
    ISBN 978-0-374-18056-0 (hardcover)
    1. Marriage—Fiction.   2. Family—Fiction.
    3. Domestic fiction.   I. Title.

PR9275.A583 K56384 2013
813'.54—dc23
                                        2012029932

Paperback ISBN: 978-0-374-53436-3

Designed by Jonathan D. Lippincott

www.fsgbooks.com
www.twitter.com/fsgbooks • www.facebook.com/fsgbooks

P1

For Candace King Weir

SEE
NOW
THEN

1

See now then, the dear Mrs. Sweet who lived with her husband Mr. Sweet and their two children, the beautiful Persephone and the young Heracles in the Shirley Jackson house, which was in a small village in New England. The house, the Shirley Jackson house, sat on a knoll, and from a window Mrs. Sweet could look down on the roaring waters of the Paran River as it fell furiously and swiftly out of the lake, a man-made lake, also named Paran; and looking up, she could see surrounding her, the mountains named Bald and Hale and Anthony, all part of the Green Mountain Range; and she could see the firehouse where sometimes she could attend a civic gathering and hear her government representative say something that might seriously affect her and the well-being of her family or see the firemen take out the fire trucks and dismantle various parts of them and put the parts back together and then polish all the trucks and then drive them around the village with a lot of commotion before putting them away again in the firehouse and they reminded Mrs. Sweet of the young Heracles, for he often did such things with his toy fire trucks; but just now when Mrs. Sweet was looking out from a window in the Shirley Jackson house, her son no longer did that. From that window again, she could see the house where the man who invented time-lapse photography lived but he was dead now; and she could see the house, the Yellow House, that Homer had restored so carefully and lovingly, polishing the floors, painting the walls, replacing the pipes, all this in the summer before that awful fall, when he went hunting and after shooting with his bow and arrow the largest deer he had ever shot, he dropped down dead while trying to load it onto the back of his truck. And Mrs. Sweet did see him lying in his coffin in the Mahar funeral home, and she thought then, why does a funeral home always seem so welcoming, so inviting from the outside, so comfortable are the chairs inside, the beautiful golden glow of the lamplight softly embracing every object in the room, the main object being the dead, why is this so, Mrs. Sweet said to herself as she saw Homer, lying all alone and snug in his coffin, and he was all dressed up in brand-new hunting clothes, a red and black plaid jacket made of boiled wool and a red knitted hat, all clothing made by Woolrich or Johnson Bros. or some outdoor clothing outfitters like that; and Mrs. Sweet wanted to speak to him, for he looked so much like himself, to ask him if he would come to paint her house, the Shirley Jackson house, or could he come and do something, anything, fix the pipes, clean the gutters of the roof, check to see if water had leaked into the basement, because he appeared to be so like himself, but his wife said to her, Homer shot the biggest deer of his life and he died while trying to put it in the back of his truck; and Mrs. Sweet was sympathetic to the worldly-ness of the dead, for she could make herself see the army of worms, parasites, who had, without malice aforethought, begun to feed on Homer and would soon reduce him to the realm of wonder and disillusion so sad, so sad all of this that Mrs. Sweet could see then, while standing at the window of the house in which Shirley Jackson had lived and across the way was the house in which old Mrs. McGovern had died and she had lived in it for many years before she became old, she had lived in her house, built in a neoclassical-something style that harkened back from another era, long ago, long before Mrs. McGovern had been born and then became a grown-up woman who married and lived with her husband in the Yellow House and made a garden of only peonies, big white ones that were streaked with a wine-dark red on the petals nearest the stamens, like an imagined night crossing an imagined day, so had been those peonies in Mrs. McGovern's garden and she had grown other things but no one could remember what they were, only her peonies were committed to memory and when Mrs. McGovern had died and so therefore vanished from the face of the earth, Mrs. Sweet had dug up those peonies from that garden, "Festiva Maxima" was their name, and planted them in her own garden, a place Mr. Sweet and the beautiful Persephone and even the young Heracles hated. The Pembrokes, father and son, mowed the lawn, though sometimes the father went off to Montpelier, the capital, to cast votes for or against, as he felt to be in the best interest of the people who lived in that village in New

England, which even now is situated on the banks of the river Paran; and the other people in that village, the Woolmingtons lived always in their house, and the Atlases too, and so also were the Elwells, the Elkinses, the Powerses; the library was full of books but no one went into it, only parents with their children, parents who wanted their children to read books, as if reading books *were* a mysterious form of love, a mystery that must remain so. The small village in New England held all that and much more and all that and much more was then and now, time and space intermingling, becoming one thing, all in the mind of Mrs. Sweet.

•

All that was visible to Mrs. Sweet as she stood in the window, at the window, but so much was not visible to her then, it lay before her, all clear and still, as if trapped on a canvas, enclosed in a rectangle made up of dead branches of *Betula nigra*, and she could not see it and could not understand it even if she could see it: her husband, the dear Mr. Sweet, hated her very much. He so often wished her dead: once then, a night when he had returned home after performing a piano concerto by Shostakovich to an audience of people who lived in the nearby villages and so felt that they wanted to get out of their homes from time to time, but as soon as they left their homes they wanted to return immediately, for nothing was nearby and nothing was as nice as their own homes and hearing Mr. Sweet play the piano made them sleepy, their heads sometimes suddenly falling forward, and they struggled to keep their chins from landing on their chests and that happened anyway and there would be lurching and balancing and gulping and coughing and though Mr. Sweet's back was turned away from his rural audience he could sense all this and he could feel every twitch, every shudder, as it registered in each individual. He loved Shostakovich and as he played the music written by this man—"The Oath to the People's Commissar," "Song of the Forests," "Eight Preludes for Piano"—the grave sorrows and injustices visited on him flowed over Mr. Sweet and he was very moved by the man and the music that the man made and he wept as he played, pouring all of his feelings of despair into that music, imagining that his life, his precious life was being spent with that dreadful woman, his wife, the dear Mrs. Sweet, who loved making three courses of French food for her small children and loved their company and she loved gardens and loved him and he was least worthy of her love, for he was such a small man, sometimes people mistook him for a rodent, he scurried around so. And he was not a rodent at all, he was a man capable of understanding Wittgenstein and Einstein and any other name that ended in stein, Gertrude included, the intricacies of the universe itself, the intricacies of human existence itself, the seeing of Now being Then and how Then becomes Now; how well he knew everything but he could not express himself, he could not show the world, at least as the world turned up in the form of the population of some small villages in New England, what a remarkable person he was then and had been and in time to come, these people who wore the same socks days in a row and didn't dye their hair after it lost the natural color and the luster it had when they were young and they liked to eat foods that were imperfect, food made limp by natural pathogens or insects for instance, people who worried about the pilot light going out of the boiler and the pipes freezing because the house was cold and then the plumber would have to be called and that plumber would complain about the work of the plumber who came before him because plumbers always found each other's work imperfect; and his audience worried about all sorts of things Mr. Sweet had never heard of because he grew up in a city and lived in a large building that had many apartments in it and when things went wrong, someone named the Super was called to make it right: the Super could change a lightbulb, get the elevator to work again after it had ceased to do so, make the garbage disappear, scrub the floor of the lobby, call the utility company if the utility company had to be called, the super could do many things and in Mr. Sweet's life, when he was a child, the super did them and Mr. Sweet had never heard of them until he came to live with that dreadful woman whom he had married and was now the mother of his children, the mother of his beautiful daughter in particular. The piano concerto came to an end and Mr. Sweet shook himself out of the deep sympathy he felt for the composer of the music and the audience shook themselves into their duck-feather-filled coats, which had trapped the smell of wood smoke from the fires built in fireplaces and wood-burning stoves, that was a winter smell, that was a smell Mr. Sweet hated, the super would have taken care of that smell, this was not a smell of Mr. Sweet's childhood; a dining room in the

Plaza Hotel, his mother wearing French perfume, those were the smells of Mr. Sweet's childhood and that then: the mother's perfume, the Plaza Hotel. And he said a good night to those people who smelled as if they lived in rooms where wood was always burning in the wood-stove, and immediately no longer thought of them as they drove home in their Subarus and secondhand Saabs, and he put on his coat, a coat made from the hair of camels, a very nice coat, double-breasted, that the beastly wife of his, Mrs. Sweet, had bought for him from Paul Stuart, a fine haberdasher in the city where Mr. Sweet was born and he hated the coat because his benighted wife had given it to him and how could she know what a fine garment it was, she who had just not long ago gotten off the banana boat, or some other benighted form of trans-port, everything about her being so benighted, even the vessel on which she arrived, and he loved the coat for it suited him, he was a prince, a prince should wear such a coat, an elegant coat; and so glad he was to be rid of this audience, he slipped behind the wheel of his own used Saab, a better one than most of the others, and he turned into a lane and then turned left onto another lane and after one quarter of a mile he could see his home, the Shirley Jackson house, the structure that held within it his doom, that prison and the guard inside, in bed already, most likely, surrounded by catalogs of flowers and their seeds, or just lying there reading *The Iliad* or *The Library of Greek My-thology* by Apollodorus, his wife that horrible bitch who'd arrived on a banana boat, it was Mrs. Sweet. But what if a surprise awaited him just inside the door, for even a poor unfortunate man as he, for so Mr. Sweet thought of himself, unfortunate to be married to that bitch of woman born of beast; the surprise being the head of his wife just lying on the counter, her body never to be found, but her head severed from it, evidence that she could no longer block his progress in the world, for it was her presence in his life that kept him from being who he really was, who he really was, who he really was, and who might that really be, for he was a man small in stature and he really felt his small stature so keenly, especially when standing beside the young Heracles, whose deeds were known and they were great and he was famous for them, even before he was born.

•

Ah, no, no! Mrs. Sweet, looking out at the mountains named Green and Anthony, and the river Paran—its man-made lake interrupting its smooth flow—in the valley, all that remained of a great geologic upheaval, a Then that she was seeing Now and her present will be buried deep in it, so deep that it will never, would never be recognized by anyone who resembled her in any shape or form: not race, not gender, not animal, not vegetable nor any of the other kingdoms, for nothing yet known can or will benefit from her suffering, and all of her existence was suffering: love, love, and love in all its forms and configurations, hatred being one of them, and yes, Mr. Sweet did love her, his hatred being a form of his love for her: see the way he admired the way her long neck would emerge from her crooked spine and bent shoulders; her legs were too long, her torso too short; her nostrils flared out like a deflated tent and came to rest on her wide fat cheeks; her ears appeared just where ears should be but then disappeared unexpectedly and if an account of them had to be made for evidence of any kind, memory of ears known in one way or another would have to be brought forth; her lips were like a child's drawing of the earth before creation, a symbol of chaos, the thing not yet knowing its true form: and that was just her physical entity, as if imagining her as something assembled in a vase decorating a table set for lunch or dinner to be eaten by people who wrote articles for magazines, or who wrote books on the fate of the very earth itself, or who wrote about the way we live now, whoever we may be, just our tiny selves nothing more nor less. But no matter, hate being a variant of love, for love is the standard and all other forms of emotion are only forms that refer to love, hatred being the direct opposite and so being its most like form: Mr. Sweet hated his wife, Mrs. Sweet, and as she looked out on this natural formation of landscape: mountain, valley, lake, and river, the remains of the violence of the earth's natural evolution: she did not know it. "Sweetie, would you like me to . . . ," was the beginning of many sentences that were expressions of love for the dear Mrs. Sweet, for she was so dear to him, and Mr. Sweet would replenish her depleted glasses of ginger ale and many segments of oranges piled on a saucer for her as she lay in the bathtub filled with hot water trying to fortify herself against the horrid something called Winter, a season really, but it was not a thing that Mrs. Sweet had ever heard of in her life preceding the banana boat, ah the banana boat, the seat of her diminishment, ah! and so did Mr. Sweet present to her the fruit, the orange, native to the earth's heated belt as she lay in hot water in a bathtub in the Shirley Jackson house. Aaaahhhh, a sweet sigh, and that would be a sound escaping through the thick, chaotic lips of Mrs. Sweet, though sound itself never escapes, for it has no place to go but out into the thin nothingness that is beyond human existence, into something Mrs. Sweet cannot now or then see. But Mr. Sweet loved her and she loved him, her love for him goes without saying now or then, it was implied, it was taken for granted, like the mountains Green and Anthony, like the man-made lake called Paran and like the river so named.

What is the essence of Love? But that was a question for Mr. Sweet, for he grew up in the atmosphere of questions of life and death: the murder of millions of people in a short period of time who lived continents away from each other; on the other hand hovering over Mrs. Sweet, though she had been made to understand it as if it were a style of a skirt, or the style of the shape of a blouse, a collar, a sleeve, was a monstrosity, a distortion of human relationships: The Atlantic Slave Trade. What is the Atlantic? What is the slave trade? So asked Mr. Sweet, and he watched Mrs. Sweet, for she was at the window that looked out at the mountains named after Green and Anthony and the river named Paran and he was returning from an auditorium that was built to seat three hundred people and only ten or twenty people had been in those seats when he was sitting at the piano playing the music written by a man who was a citizen of Russia who wrote this music that so captivated the very soul, whatever that may be, of Mr. Sweet was in distress, knowing and yet not knowing death itself in all its not-knownness. What is the essence of Love?

But Mrs. Sweet was looking out at her life: from the Shirley Jackson house, across the way lay the mountains Green and Anthony and laying beneath them were the rivers: Paran and Battenkill and Branch, bodies of water, full of trout hungry for a midafternoon hatch of invertebrates, and all these rivers flow into the Hudson River, a body of water, one of many tributaries to that larger body of water, the Atlantic Ocean, all of them flowing there except for the Mettowee which flows into Lake Champlain; and she was thinking of her now, knowing that it would most certainly become a Then even as it was a Now, for the present will be now then and the past is now then and the future will be a now then, and that the past and the present and the future has no permanent present tense, has no certainty in regard to right now, and she gathered up her children, the young Heracles who would always be so, no matter what befell him, and the beautiful Persephone, who would always be so, beautiful and perfect and just.

•

But her head was not lying on the yellow kitchen counter, severed from her body, with the rest of her scattered into time: her torso preserved in mud near the Delaware Water Gap, her legs in a granite outcrop in the Ahaggar massif, her hands in the shifting sands of the Imperial Sand Dunes, and an exquisite sight are all these presentations to be found in that thing called Nature but Mr. Sweet could never see this, for it frightened him to leave his familiar surroundings, the Shirley Jackson house and all the nice furnishings in it: the sofa and chairs that were covered in cloth that Mrs. Sweet had purchased at the Waverley factory outlet in Adams, Massachusetts, and the upholstery itself, which had been done by a man who lived in White Creek, New York. He made a nest-like space for himself in the room above the garage, a studio in which he wrote many things, and it looked like a replica of the welcome area of a funeral home, so thought Mrs. Sweet and that thought almost killed her; but he loved that room, for it was dark and full of all sorts of things that he loved, his memories of Paris, France, deviled eggs, his many collections of the Claudine books, the picture of the little girl he asked to undress when they were both six years old, the picture of his student he was in love with when she was seventeen and he was twenty-seven, the puppets he made when he was a child, the delicious puddings he ate when he was a little child, the old stubs of tickets from the city ballet, the old stubs of tickets from the theater, all little mementos from a time so precious to him: his childhood; but she was such a beast, such a bitch and a beast and she must not be allowed anywhere near this room and he kept it locked and she was never allowed in it and he kept the key with him all the time, except when he got into bed with her, he placed it in a secret place, a place so secret that he never thought of it, for fear she might read his thoughts. Who knew what she was capable of? People who come on banana boats are not people you can really know and she did come on a banana boat. All the same her head was not lying on the kitchen counter and the kitchen counter was covered in yellow Formica, an idea very revolting to

Mr. Sweet, for a kitchen counter should be white or marble or just plain wood but Mrs. Sweet would go out of her way to find such an abomination, yellow Formica, to cover the counter and then she would paint the wall in the kitchen those Caribbean colors: mango, pineapple, not peaches and nectarine: "My house looks like the house of someone my dear mother, who warned me not to marry this horrible bitch, my dear mother who could see right away that we were not compatible, my dear, dear mother, who warned me against taking up with this woman of no proper upbringing but I loved her legs, they were so long, she could wrap them around me twice and still they did not touch the ground, those legs that are now buried in an outcropping of rocks in a place I can never visit; and I loved the way she could exaggerate, so that if she saw ten tulips in a vase, she would say she saw ten thousand daffodils at a glance, tossing their heads in sprightly dance; she would sometimes put a rainbow in the sky, just because it was a beautiful day but she thought it should be more so and a rainbow would be just the thing, it was so amusing and so different, she went everywhere and then she would come back and tell me about everywhere and I knew she embellished, not really lied, it's just that nothing was ever the way she said: the woods in Connecticut were not beautiful at all, they were full of bloodsucking flies that left huge welts where they had bit you; and I didn't want to live in this godforsaken village, where at least three women have left their husbands for other women and I am sure eventually she'll be one of them, though I don't wish her on anybody; I didn't want to live in a village where a man left his wife to become a woman so he could marry another woman, someone entirely different from his wife; I didn't want to live in a place where everyone is so fat and everyone is related to everyone else and the women are not beautiful at all and I am so grateful for my lovely young female students, whom I fall in love with, I am not ashamed to say, though I would never say it out loud, I never speak very loud, and another thing to hate about her, she is very loud, loud, loud! I don't want to come home to Aretha Franklin all the time, I didn't want to live in a place where the day ended at five in the afternoon in January and eight in the evening in July and teach at a school where the singing teacher cannot sing and the other teachers are stupid; I hate this place, this village, I never wanted to live here, I have always lived in a city, a place where people are civilized and where it is frowned upon to have a child with your sister or your brother, a place where people go to the theater, they go to movies made by François Truffaut, *The 400 Blows* makes them laugh to themselves, distracting them from the fact that there is not a taxi to be found on upper Fifth Avenue when you want one; she dragged me here that stupid bitch who arrived on a banana boat and my mother warned me against marrying her, we had then nothing in common and we have now nothing in common. She dragged me here, she said the children would be better off: the air is fresh, the air is fresh but I hate fresh air and all those trees, all those trees, losing their leaves, gaining their leaves again just when I thought they were dead, for I love dead trees, I love tall buildings made to look as if they were made from granite or something indestructible, something eternal, something that will always be there, a city never sleeps, there is always someone who is doing something and can never sleep and there they will be keeping alive to me the idea that to be alive is to be forever in touch with something that never ceases to be itself, that never takes a pause, that while I am asleep the business of living persists; but not her, she loves the life cycle, or so she says, though it is such an ugly way of presenting a beautiful idea: the life cycle but she is an ugly person, a bitch and an ugly person, her existence makes me sick, her name is not Lulu, her name is Mrs. Sweet and she is not that; and the children would love the fresh air and these children, I had no idea of them, I could want them or not want them, one day she said the children would like the fresh air: the children would like the fresh air. I hate fresh air, the idea of it, fresh air does not have Duke Ellington and I love Duke Ellington and often as a child, sitting in my bedroom alone, I imagined myself to be Duke Ellington, domineering and dominating my orchestra filled with brilliant musicians on the various horns and drums and then composing grand pieces of music that would never be received with respect and recognized as the works of genius that they are, then and now, the equal of Alban Berg and Arnold Schoenberg and Anton Webern and this fills me with despair, for I see myself as Duke Ellington and I see myself as Alban, Anton, Arnold. And in this Shirley Jackson house, nestled in the crotch of the prison of a village in New England, I now live with that passenger, questionable passenger, on a banana boat, for is she a passenger or is she a banana? If she was a banana was she inspected? If she was a passenger, how did she get here? My mother was right: someone who arrives on a banana boat is suspect; to eat bananas in January is strange and a luxury. In any case, in winter, as a boy I ate Rice Krispies with sliced bananas for breakfast while sitting at the foot of my parents' bed and the bananas had no taste that I can remember, they were bananas, a constant and an inevitability like the elevator arriving when I pushed a button that summoned it or like the maid being condescended to by my mother; in any case, life is a series of inevitabilities; in any case, one day my mother died and before that, my father died and I was all alone."

•

Now and Then, Mrs. Sweet said to herself, though this was done only in her mind's eye, as she stood at the window, unmindful of the rage and hatred and utter disdain that her beloved Mr. Sweet nurtured in his small breast for her, now and then, seeing it as it presented itself, a series of tableaux. The mountains Green and Anthony, the lake, the river, the valley that lay spread out before her, all serene in their seeming permanence, all created by forces that answered to no known existence, were a refuge from that tormented landscape that made up Mrs. Sweet's fifty-two-year-old inner life. No morning arrived in all its freshness, its newness, bearing no trace of all the billions of mornings that had come before, that Mrs. Sweet didn't think, first thing, of the turbulent waters of the Caribbean Sea and the Atlantic Ocean. She thought of that landscape before she opened her eyes and the thoughts surrounding that landscape made her open her eyes. Her eyes, dark, impenetrable Mr. Sweet would say, as he looked into them, at first he said the word impenetrable with delight, for he thought of discovering something not yet known to him, something that lay in Mrs. Sweet's eyes and that would make him free, free, free from all that bound him, and then he cursed her dark eyes, for they offered him nothing; in any case his own eyes were blue and Mrs. Sweet was indifferent to that particular feature of his. But Mrs. Sweet's eyes were not impenetrable at all to anyone else and everyone she met wished that they were so; for behind her eyes lay scenes of turbulence, upheavals, murders, betrayals, on foot, on land, and on the seas where horde upon horde of people were transported to places on the earth's surface that they had never heard of or even imagined, and murderer and murdered, betrayer and betrayed, the source of the turbulence, the instigator of the upheavals, were all mixed up, and the sorting out of the true, true truth and the rendering of judgments, or the acceptance of wrongs, and to accept that, to accept and lay still with being wronged will wear you down to nothing so that eventually you are not more than the substance that makes up the Imperial Sand Dunes in the Imperial Valley in California, or the pink beaches surrounding the rising shelf of landmass that is now, just now, the island of Barbuda, or the lawn of a house in Montclair, New Jersey. But those eyes of hers were not a veil to her soul, someone so substantial, so vivid, so full of the thing called life did not need a veil for she was her soul and her soul was herself; and her childhood and her youth and middle age, all of her was intact and complete; all of her,

all of her, was not exempt from Imperial Sand Dunes or
beaches on emerging landmasses or lawns in New Jersey,
not so, not so, but all the same when she opened her eyes
each morning that seemed not to know of the mornings
that had come before, her now and her then was seen in
the human light and she saw herself with tenderness and
sympathy and even love, yes love, and turning her body,
she saw next to her, Mr. Sweet: his hair vanishing, each
strand forever lost one day at a time, a thin layer of dan-
druff covering his scalp and trapped in the thread-
straight locks of the remaining hair, his breath perfumed
by a properly digested dinner he had enjoyed the night
before, but she did not see his disappointments: *The
Albany Symphony, The Four Quartets, The Music Teacher.*
Mrs. Sweet's eyes could see Mrs. Sweet very well in the
little room off to the side of the kitchen and in that place
she came alive in all her tenses, then, now, then again
and she was in the little room off the kitchen and she sat
at the desk that Donald had made for her and placed her
hands on a tablet of writing paper.

•

And getting a mere glimpse of her in that pose, sitting
humbly as if she were at the Moravian school in Points
and before her was a copy of the Nelson West Indian
Reader and at the desk that Donald had made for her,
her hands on a tablet of writing paper, made Mr. Sweet
sigh in despair, for in truth, everyone, anyone, in the
whole world knew that he was the true heir of the position of sitting at the desk and contemplating the blank

mound of sheets of paper, and in a state of rage he walked up to his studio, situated above the garage of the Shirley Jackson house, and he sat down at his piano, and this was not made by Donald who had taken up carpentry as a hobby and so it was in that spirit, the spirit of love and free of worldly worth, he had made Mrs. Sweet that desk; Mr. Sweet's piano was made by Steinway. And Mr. Sweet struck a chord but no one could hear it, not anyone in the garage, there was no one in the garage, no one could hear him but he could hear the sound of the washing machine washing the clothes of his infernal family and in that entity he did not include himself: the children's clothes, his wife's gardening clothes, his wife's underwear, the table linen for Mrs. Sweet would not allow them to use paper napkins, the sheets and the pillowcases, the bath mats, the kitchen towels, the bath towels, all sorts of things had to be washed and he had never thought of things being washed, except when he was a student in Paris, France, and Cambridge, Massachusetts, and his things got washed but his things being washed didn't interfere with the striking of a chord. And now, so different from then; and then was a struggle and now the struggle would lead to his death; how happy, he thought to himself, to be alone, away from that woman who could and would walk into a room all by herself and sit at a desk Donald had made for her, and there she would think about her childhood, the misery that resulted from that wound, eventually becoming its own salve, from the wound itself, she made a world and this world that she had made out of her own horror was full of interest and was even attractive. To be away from her, this woman, now my wife, but then when I first met her, just a very thin girl, like a strayed branch of a stray tree waiting for the pruning shears or a weed, nothing to be given a second thought as it was pulled out of the way for it interfered with something of real beauty and value; oh yes, how happy to be away from that woman, he was thinking and talking to himself of Mrs. Sweet, who could find the death of Homer a source of endless wonder, a man who had repaired a house in which they lived, seeing him dead and lying in his coffin, wearing his hunting clothes, just bought from the store and looking as if at any moment he would sit up and say something that would not be agreeable to Mr. Sweet but Mrs. Sweet would say it was so interesting and amazing: how amazing, was something she liked to say, and she said it about the simplest thing: a rainbow, for instance; three rainbows, one after the other, at the same time, as if drawn by a child who would be regarded with suspicion in any culture in any part of the world at any given time in human existence; as if it were the first time such a thing had appeared before; so Amazing, she says, would say, so said Mr. Sweet to himself, in his studio above the garage, and in the garage, to accommodate him, to prevent him from hearing any sounds that were not made by him, no cars were allowed. All the same, he could hear the dunning sound caused by the washing machine and the clothes dryer and the hub-hub of the household beyond: Mr. Pembroke is mowing the lawn, the heating oil man from Green Oil is filling up the heating oil tank, Blue Flame Gas is here to fill up those gas tanks, the man from CVPS is reading the meter, the furnace has just broken down even though it is only five years old, the young Heracles has tonsillitis, the beautiful Persephone hates her mother Mrs. Sweet, Mrs. Sweet now looks exactly like Charles Laughton as he portrayed Captain Bligh in the film *Mutiny on the Bounty*, a girl student of Mr. Sweet would like to talk to him about his thoughts on *Pierrot Lunaire* over a glass of Pimm's Cup in Mrs. Sweet's garden, for that girl so loves gardens and perhaps Mr. Sweet so loves that girl. But that dunning sound, said Mr. Sweet to himself, and looking out, just then, of a window in the beautiful studio that Mrs. Sweet had insisted be built for him, so he could be isolated from the children who might be in a room next door and, while there, want to construct a creature from some material bought at Kmart that was meant to resemble the makeup of a being that was imagined and yet even so looked like something familiar, and the children, the beautiful Persephone and the young Heracles, beautiful and young, were so loud, so loud, and they would only get louder and Mr. Sweet could only wish them louder, for anything other than louder was unbearable and would kill even him. Yes, Mr. Sweet was so sad, for he had married and made the mother of his children, a woman who loved living in a small village in New England, a place where a man, who went hunting deer every autumn of his life, died in the midst of securing one of them onto the back of his truck, and it all made this woman he had come to regard as dreadful, like something in a tale read without thinking to children just before they went to bed, children whose fears had a source that was not properly known to them: The Brothers Grimm! Oh God! *The Runaway Bunny*! *Harold and the Purple Crayon*! *Goodnight Moon*! *The*

Tale of Two Bad Mice! The Tailor of Gloucester! The Tale of Peter Rabbit! Where the Wild Things Are! Yes, Mr. Sweet was so sad, for he had married and made the mother of his children a woman who knew all sorts of things but she did not know him, that would be Mr. Sweet, but who could know such a person as this man, who carried himself not as a man, but as a rodent from that era, the Mesozoic, when the first mammals took that shape.

And then there in that room that was just above the garage and in spite of the infernal sounds coming from the big white metal boxes that served to make clothes clean, Mr. Sweet composed his nocturnes, for he only loved nocturnes, and this one he called *This Marriage Is Dead* and he placed all manner of rage in it and that rage was true and justified, for look, see, just out the window, outside, the young Heracles, a small boy just then, arranging his collection of shy Myrmidons, gifts tucked away in Happy Meals purchased from McDonalds, and he had no interest in the meal itself, only he wanted to collect the small plastic warriors who were made to look like the followers of a hero of the Trojan War; and now he was arranging them and rearranging them and making an imaginary storm descend on them, scattering them all over the green lawn which he made into an imaginary sea, and as the shy Myrmidons drowned again, coming to rest, legs in the air, held up by the blades of grass that would soon require cutting by Mr. Pembroke, Mr. Sweet set these scenes of battles and drowning to the music that made up the nocturne, *This Marriage Is Dead*, though sometimes he changed the title to *This Marriage Has Been Dead for a Long Time Now*. Oh, such wailing and gnashing of teeth, such beating of breast, so many tears were cried that it could have made a roaring river and you could have built a boat and sailed down into the ocean on it and looking back to see the wending ways of that river, you could give that river a name, so thought Mrs. Sweet, one day, one day when she first heard those words This Marriage Is Dead, This Marriage Has Been Dead for a Long Time Now, though not when she first heard them as a nocturne performed in an auditorium, one night in winter, surrounded by friends and loved ones and clutching the hand of the young Heracles, for she had wanted him to hear his father's music, for she had wanted him to think that his father loved him, for she had wanted him to think that his father loved her, for she had wanted a great deal too much; that time when she first heard that nocturne, she could see Dan revving the engine of the old Volvo, which was stopped at the red light in front of the Coop in the square, next to a Porsche, and the driver of the Porsche was offended by the noise of the Volvo and when the red light changed to green, he sped ahead and Dan and the young Heracles stayed in place and laughed at him and they did not know who that driver was and they did not wonder if that driver knew of them, they only laughed and laughed.

But all that aside, for all that would have its then and has its own now, Mr. Sweet sitting on a stool in the studio above the garage, the dun-dun, wooo-wooo, whoosh-whoosh noise made by the clothes-cleaning machines, and he sat there, hovered above the black and white keys of that musical instrument made by the company called Steinway, his hands poised above those keys, his fingers extended, his fingers resembling his long-ago ancestors who lived in that long-ago era, and he composed more nocturnes, more nocturnes, and more of those: his life was not what he wanted it to be, not what he had imagined it to be even though he had not imagined it to be anything in particular other than he would be princely and entitled to doormen and poor but princely and entitled to doormen and sad because he loved ballet and Wittgenstein and opera and entitled to doormen, no matter what, there must be doormen. But now, there just outside as he looked out the window, was the young Heracles saying, Dad, Dad, and the young Heracles was playing golf now, imagining himself a champion and wearing a silly jacket in a specific shade of the color green, or a champion of something or the other and Mr. Sweet did loathe all that the boy enjoyed and would never, ever take him to the Basketball Hall of Fame in Springfield, Massachusetts, but he would have taken him to the home of Dmitri Shostakovich if it was in Springfield, Massachusetts, and he wanted that boy, the young Heracles, dead and he wanted another boy, who could sit still in the movie theater watching a cartoon, and not need Adderall or any kind of stimulant that made you still, to take his place, and that someone saying, Dad! Dad! could be a boy who was alive even in stillness; but then, years later, now, now, now, the young Heracles, when asked to look back on the wreckage that had been made of his young life by those words which had become the title of a song, a book, a recipe for a kind of sponge cake, directions for removing stains left by food spilled on the front of your dress or shirt while feeding the baby, turning left when your spouse is certain you should have turned right: *This Marriage Is Dead* or sometimes known as *The Marriage Is Dead* and sometimes, when it has been reduced to a folk song, is called *Husband Left Her*, when asked about it in this way: "What now, young Heracles, for your life was such a wreck, but now it must look like an accident, a bunch of stuff all over the place, seen in the rearview mirror"; and the young Heracles, without pause, replied, "Yes, but objects in the mirror are closer than they appear."

And so too, without pause, then and now, the dead marriage grew into a loud, beastly entity that could be seen dancing on the lawn just within view of Mr. Sweet as he sat in the room above the garage, writing and rewriting the nocturne itself, its arms touching the tops of the Taconic range in the west, its legs mixing freely with the boreal forest in the east, hovering above the various waterways named Hudson, Battenkill, Walloomsac, Hoosic, Mettowee, that lay in between. The dead marriage occupied each empty space that was innocently bare in that village in which the Sweets lived, even in the post office, where the postmistress looked at Mrs. Sweet with pity and scorn before handing her a notice of an overdue bill; so too, it was alive in the country store, for when Mrs. Sweet entered the premises all conversation stopped, and everyone looked at her with pity and scorn and perhaps were sorry that none of them had an overdue bill to hand to her, and perhaps were happy that none of them had an overdue bill for her and Mrs. Sweet purchased some cheese and yogurt made by Mrs. Burley.

That nocturne *This Marriage Is Dead* or *The Marriage Has Been Dead for a Long Time Now*, or the popular folk song *Husband Left Her*, brought such joy to Mr. Sweet and he felt, for the first time in his life, fulfilled; his whole life had been lived, all his suffering for his whole life had ceased just then, for he had suffered much: the life of a prince, when he was a child and lived in an apartment across from that specially arranged plantation of greenness in New York City, Central Park, overwhelmed his whole being and he reached into the pocket of his tweed jacket, which bore the label of J. Press, a haberdasher on Madison Avenue and East Forty-sixth Street and he found a piece of paper, a note and he read it with the surprise of the new and he read it with the familiarity with which you say to yourself, in whatever incarnation you find yourself: child, adolescent, twenties, thirties, middle age, old, in a hospice hours before your heart becomes still, yes! Tell now, Tell then, the note had nothing written on it and the note had this written on it: This is how to live your life, and it was signed, Your Father.

Her hands now holding a pencil, Mrs. Sweet began to write on the pages before her:

"It is true that my mother loved me very much, so much that I thought love was the only emotion and even the only thing that existed; I only knew love then and I was an infant up to the age of seven and could not know that love itself, though true and a stable standard, is more varied and unstable than any element or substance that rises up from the earth's core; my mother loved me and I did not know that I should love her in return; it never occurred to me that she would grow angry at me for not returning the love she gave to me; I accepted the love she gave me without a thought to her and took it for my own right to live in just the way that would please me; and then my mother became angry at me because I did not love her in return and then she became even more angry that I did not love her at all because I would not become her, I had an idea that I should become myself; it made her angry that I should have a self, a separate being that could never be known to her; she taught me to read and she was very pleased at how naturally I took to it, for she thought of reading as a climate and not everyone adapts to it; she did not know that before she taught me to read I knew how to write, she did not know that she herself was writing and that once I knew how to read I would then write about her; she wished me dead but not into eternity, she wished me dead at the end of day and that in the morning she would give birth to me again; in a small room of the public library of St. John's, Antigua, she showed me books about the making of the earth, the workings of the human digestive system, the causes of some known diseases, the lives of some European composers of classical music, the meaning of pasteurization; I cannot remember that I was taught the alphabet, the letters A B and C one after the other in sequence with all the others ending in the letter Z, I can only see now that those letters formed into words and that the words themselves leapt up to meet my eyes and that my eyes then fed them to my lips and so between the darkness of my impenetrable eyes and my lips that are the shape of chaos before the tyranny of order is imposed on them is where I find myself, my true self and from that I write; but I knew how to write before I could read, for all that I would write about had existed before my knowing how to read and transport it into words and put it down on paper, and all of the world had existed before I even knew how to speak of it, had existed before I even knew how to understand it, and in looking at it even more closely, I don't really know how to write because there is so much before me that I cannot yet read; I cannot write why I did not love my mother then when she loved me so completely; what I felt for her has no name that I can now find; I thought her love for me and her own self was one thing and that one thing was my own, completely my own, so much so that I was part of what was my own and I and my own were inseparable and so to love my mother was not known to me and so her anger directed toward me was incomprehensible to us both; my mother taught me to read, she and I at first could read together and then she and I could read separately but not be in conflict, but then, to see it now, only I would write; after she taught me to read, I caused such disruption in my mother's everyday life: I asked her for more books and she had none to give me and so she sent me to a school that I would only be allowed in and admitted to if I was five years old; I was already taller than was expected for someone my age, three and a half years old, and my mother said to me, now remember when they ask you how old say you are five, over and over again, she made me repeat that I was five and when the teacher asked me how old I was I said that I was five years of age and she believed me; it is perhaps then that I became familiar with the idea that knowing how to read could alter my circumstances, that then I came to know that the truth could be unstable while a lie is hard and dark, for it was not a lie to say that I was five when I was three and a half years old, for three and a half years old then was now, and my five-year-old self then would soon be in my now; that teacher's name was Mrs. Tanner and she was a very large woman, so large that she could not turn around quickly and we would take turns pinching her bottom, and by the time she looked to see which of us had done so we would assume a pose of innocence and she never knew which one of us had been so rude and mischievous; and it was while in Mrs. Tanner's presence that I came to develop fully my two selves, then and now, united only through seeing, and it happened in this way: Mrs. Tanner was teaching us to read from a book with simple words and pictures, but since I already knew how to read I could see things within the book that I was not meant to see; the story in the book was about a man who was a farmer and his name was Mr. Joe and he had a dog named Mr. Dan and a cat named Miss Tibbs and a cow who did not have a name, the cow was only called the cow, and he had a hen and her name was Mother Hen and she had twelve chicks, eleven of them were ordinary, golden chicks, but the twelfth one was bigger than the others and had black feathers and he had a name, it was Percy; Percy caused his mother a great deal of worry, for he always would provoke the anger of Miss Tibbs and Mr. Dan by attempting to eat their food; but his mother's greatest worry came when she saw him try to fly up to sit on the uppermost bar of the farm's fence; he tried and tried and failed and then one day succeeded but only for a moment and then he fell down and broke one of his wings and one of his legs; it was Mr. Joe who said, 'Percy the chick had a fall.' I liked that sentence then and I like that sentence now but then I had no way of making any sense of it, I could only keep it in my mind's eye, where it rested and grew in the embryo that would become my imagination; a good three and a half years later, I met Percy again but in another form; as a punishment for misbehaving in class, I was made to copy Books One and Two of *Paradise Lost* by John Milton and I fell in love with Lucifer, especially as he was portrayed in the illustration, standing victoriously on one foot on a charred globe, the other foot aloft, his arms flung out in that way of the victor, brandishing a sword in one of them, his head of hair thick and alive for his hair was all snakes poised to strike; I then remembered Percy and I do now know Percy."

2

To see then Mr. Sweet, a very small boy in short pants and short-sleeved shirt bounding across the green grass of a lawn, selling, in a boyish way, water flavored with lemon juice and sugar to friends of his parents, sitting in a chair and listening to jazz, eating peaches that had been poached in pineapple juice, speaking authoritatively of being and not being, traversing the island that was Manhattan, and at that time not being able to see at all the house in which Shirley Jackson lived, the house in which he would live with the fugues trapped in his head, murdering the young Heracles over and over again and that boy coming alive again and again; to see Mr. Sweet, the short pants and short-sleeved shirt being replaced by the brown corduroy suit that Mrs. Sweet had purchased at the Brooks Brothers outlet in Manchester; not being able to see his then now; to see Mr. Sweet then before he was Mr. Sweet, innocent of the small short-haired mammal that thrived in the Mesozoic era; Mr. Sweet who was often found lying down on a couch in an old house that had once been occupied by a woman who wrote short stories and brought up her children and whose husband had betrayed her and had behaved as if he were nothing more than a louse to her, so recorded in a biography of her life.

Closing his eyes then, a long time ago now, there is Mr. Sweet, sitting at that ancient instrument, the harp, wrestling with that large triangle and holding it steady against his small, pretend manly breast; wrestling with a diminishing pitch here, a lengthening string there; gut in the middle, wire below; the flats and sharps, the major and minor keys, harmonic systems, double melodies, polyphony, monodists, melismata in the plainsong, the contrapuntal forms, allegro, concertos, not yet the nocturne—not now that but the ballad—oh yes, oh yes, all that flooded over Mr. Sweet as he sat before his ancient instrument, the harp, worshipping and worshipping, its holiness causing him to grow weak, he was so young, not yet Mr. Sweet and yet he was always Mr. Sweet as even he himself could see now then.

Oh, but this is the voice of the monodist, and with the ancient instrument Mr. Sweet is on a stage all alone, the podium has even been moved to the side, the auditorium is full of chairs but no audience, and this pleases the young Mr. Sweet, young and full-size he is then, not old and the size of a mole as he is now, and he plays the ancient instrument with joy and love and earthly vigor, so much vigor, and breaks all the strings on the ancient instrument from which now, right now, at this very moment, comes no music at all. But then, then, the auditorium is full of chairs but no people, no one at all, and tugging on the strings of the ancient instrument, with its strings made of gut and wire, Mr. Sweet plays a song, for he is not yet a theorist and he plays a song, a complete song full of harmonies and melodies so simple anyone could sing it, even the young Heracles just after Mr. Sweet has beheaded him could sing that song. *The Beheading of Heracles* was a title Mr. Sweet gave to all the music he played on the ancient instrument Then, *Sweet Night for Heracles* is the name Mr. Sweet gives the music he plays on the ancient instrument Now. And at the end of each suite or sonata, for the young Mr. Sweet plays everything in every way, each kind then was the same, there being no audience to make a distinction, chairs are indifferent, came a deafening silence, applause yes, silence all the same. An immortal to empty chairs was Mr. Sweet then, but he was a boy with all those things hammering against the inside of his head, notes and notes of music, arranging themselves into every known form but never into forms not yet known.

Oh, and this was the word Mrs. Sweet heard, that poor dear woman, mending socks upstairs. Oh, it was the voice of the monodist, her poor dear Mr. Sweet. Whack, came a sound from the young Heracles, as he made a putt, a basket, and a score and yet was under par or over par, Mrs. Sweet could never be sure. The boy's head, free of his body with its entrails, filled up all the empty chairs in the auditorium of Mr. Sweet's youthful recital. Not that, not that, cried the young Mr. Sweet and he made the chairs empty again. The strings of the harp, gut and wire, broke and he bent down and over to make the instrument well again, so ancient was this instrument. The Shirley

Jackson house was not known to him then. Never did he imagine then—his youth was his now—that he would live in such a house, so big, so full of empty spaces that were never used, never filled up even in the imagination, the young Heracles with his endless tasks of hitting balls, large and small, into holes of all sizes; the young Heracles, growing in youth, not growing older, growing in his youth, becoming more perfectly youthful, his many tasks to perform, performing them more perfectly, at first performing them awkwardly, not right at all, but then becoming so good he could place any ball of any size in any hole, no matter its width or depth or height. Thwack, was a sound caused by the quick movement of the young Heracles' hand sweeping a ball through the teeming air; whack, was the sound of his head sliced away from his body. Oh, was the sound that came out of the mouth of the monodist, Mr. Sweet, Mr. Sweet, as he saw the young Heracles pick his head off the floor and replace it on his neck, which was just above his shoulders, with such deftness, as if he were born to do only that, keep his head in that place just above shoulders.

Young Heracles, his tasks, so many, so many: wash the dishes, put them away, clean the stables, walk the horses, fix the roof, milk the cows, emerge from his mother's womb in the usual way, slay the monster, cross the river, return again, climb up the mountain, descend on the other side, build a castle on the top of a hill, imprison the innocent in a dungeon, lay waste to whole villages to the surprise of the villagers, trap and then skin the she-fox, eat his green vegetables and his meat too, kill his father, not kill his father, want to kill his father but not kill his father, keep his head on his shoulders, survive the threshold of night, await the dawn, take a pickax to the iris (his eyes, not the flowers growing in his mother's garden), seize the sun, banish the moon, at every moment his skin so cold, the fire at his back, cross the road by himself, tie his shoelaces, kiss a girl, sleep in his own bed. Ah, gee Dad, said the young Heracles, as he raced to get a glass of water from the kitchen sink to quench the unquenchable thirst he had acquired after one of his many journeys, Sorry, Sorry. The young Heracles had then collided with Mr. Sweet, hitting him squarely in the head, causing starry lights to shoot out of his ears and nostrils and eyes, sending Mr. Sweet into a coma from which he emerged many years later and immediately he cut off the young Heracles' head again. But that the young Heracles, blessed with a natural instinct to live that would never, ever abandon him, picked up his head and put it back on—again, where it rests to this day, in the rising just above his shoulders.

Oh, was the sound of the harsh sigh violently escaping the prison that was Mr. Sweet's lips, as he lay in the studio above the garage in the Shirley Jackson house. And he lay there on a brown couch, still, as if dead, but he was not dead, he only hated to be alive, with that wife, who now, now, knitted furiously, even with great vigor. Her heart raced with the effort, faster and faster and then even faster than that. Oh, so dangerously fast did her heart beat that it almost beat itself to death, but Mrs. Sweet said, gggggrrrrgghhhh, the sound of blood and oxygen combined as it simultaneously reached her throat. What the hell and oh shit, said Mrs. Sweet, and how surprised she was to hear these words catapulting out and around inside her head, for these were not her own words, these were the words of the young Heracles, the young Heracles spoke in this way when he thought no one could overhear him. But this (what the hell, oh shit) was in response to: the children—this would be the young Heracles and the beautiful Persephone—won't get out of bed in time to meet the school bus, the man who can repair the household appliances won't come on a mutually agreed time, it will rain when the sun should shine, the fruit will rot on the bushes, Mr. Sweet will not emerge from the studio above the garage as Mr. Sweet, he will emerge from the studio above the garage inside a mauve velvet-covered coffin, an imitation of a jewelry box, Mr. Sweet will be dead. This last—Mr. Sweet being dead—if Mr. Sweet was dead what would happen to Mrs. Sweet, who would she be? Mrs. Sweet was a knitter and mender of socks, and she did that because while doing so she could delineate and dissect and then examine the world as she knew it, as she understood it, as she imagined it, as it came to her through her everyday existence.

All that day, all that night, as the very thing called time collapsed within itself, Mrs. Sweet made socks and in that way marked off time, and in that way sought out the things that had not yet entered her mind. She mended and knitted away at the socks, repairing the holes, sometimes making just ordinary stitches, sometimes making a Christmas tree and a Santa Claus in the colors red and green to fill the holes, eventually undoing those to finally fill the holes with six-pointed stars and biblical scrolls in blue and white. Mr. Sweet hated this, how he hated this, the six-pointed stars and the biblical scroll in blue and white, the sight of it making him swear that he would be a deathbed Catholic, whatever could that mean, thought Mrs. Sweet, for she so loved Mr. Sweet and thought always that his contradictions were a source of laughter, whatever could that be or mean, a deathbed Catholic. But Mrs. Sweet loved Mr. Sweet without blinds.

And so it was that one day, out of the blue, now, to be exact, Mr. Sweet said to her, you have said horrible things to me and to the young Heracles and to the beautiful Persephone and to the other people that have not been yet born of you and me. On hearing that, Mrs. Sweet cried and cried, not wanting to believe that she was the kind of Mrs. Sweet who could say things that were not kind and sweet and she grew silent. On seeing her deep, black felt coat, her natural skin it was, for Mrs. Sweet by this time could from time to time be herself, Mr. Sweet wished her dead but she was so alive, mending the holes in the socks properly, filling them up sometimes, with patterns he did not like, patterns he so hated; she was so alive, when she walked down the stairs, after mending the socks, her shoulders held up and back, straight, as if they had never known burden and weight of any kind at all, no, not at all.

You have said such horrible things to me, said Mr. Sweet to Mrs. Sweet as she walked in the door of their house, the very one in which Shirley Jackson had lived, and these words were new to Mrs. Sweet's ears for she was just then returning from the synagogue with a Sweet's kind of wisdom to share with him. The rabbi had told Mrs. Sweet of a biblical interpretation. The rabbi had said that in a vision it was revealed that all the bricks made by the slaves who had built ancient Egyptian civilization held a baby within them. Inside each brick was a full baby, and the baby cried out. Inside each brick, a perfect baby was curled up, lying there and not dead, not alive, Mrs. Sweet pondered, as she mended the socks, upstairs, on another floor from the studio, and as she mended the socks, she did not think of what was imprisoned in each stitch, each stitch being a small thing in itself that would make up a whole. I shall be a deathbed Catholic, Mr. Sweet said to her, and with such hatred, thought Mrs. Sweet then, but whether directed toward the baby who lay inside that ancient brick or a priest, she could not tell. I shall be a deathbed Catholic, and as the world turned, continuing in its mysterious way, mysterious to any human being trying to understand her place in it (that would be Mrs. Sweet), his place in it (that would be Mr. Sweet), not yet the young Heracles (he was still a boy), not yet the beautiful Persephone (she was still a girl), and Mrs. Sweet turned those words over and over again in her mind.

Mr. Sweet did not hate the rabbi and did not hate Catholics, so thought Mrs. Sweet to herself. Mr. Sweet does not hate the rabbi and does not hate Catholics but he does hate me, is not what Mrs. Sweet thought to herself. Her chin sagged down to the place just beneath her breasts and then came back up to its natural setting, which at her age was at the same level as her collarbones. How wearying was Mr. Sweet and his outbursts and making things of them, thought Mrs. Sweet, but then again, no one did that anymore, no one, Meg and Rob—just for instance—

considered the outbursts, the ever-changing moods, the volatile emotions, of their companions wearying. The young Heracles asked his mother, this would be Mrs. Sweet, to make him a meal, breakfast, dinner, or something in between, and she took offense and they quarreled over this, the result was a great calm, silence even, and the calm and silence were filled up with many words.

Hear then the young Heracles, still innocent of the notions of honor and glory: Dad, he said, do you want to go bowling? But Mr. Sweet could see the bowling alley, it had in it people who had eaten more than they should and this very thing was a badge of honor, and they spoke loudly and would die of diseases that were curable, they would never die of natural causes, but what would that be, for to die is natural. But in time will come a collection of events saturated with feelings and smells and the way someone remembered them and the way something, anything, felt like, and the sounds and someone experiencing the relation between sound and time and even space—oh, oh! Oh, oh, said Mr. Sweet, do we have to, do we have to, and he could see all the people in the bowling alley, throwing bowling balls with accuracy and finding satisfaction in that, and throwing bowling balls in a carefree manner and finding equal satisfaction in that, and he hated those people, for none of them knew of adagios and B flats and symphonies and boogie-woogie and all that, they only knew of the joy of the wooden ball knocking down wooden pins in the lanes. Dad, do you want to go bowling, said the young Heracles to Mr. Sweet and Mr. Sweet said, yes, bowl you out of existence, but the young Heracles skipped away to the car, an old Volkswagen Rabbit in which they would drive to the bowling alley, and did not hear his father say those words. Just before they entered the bowling alley, Mr. Sweet fell and broke the bone in the smallest finger of his right hand and so for a short time was unable to play on the pianoforte a melody written by a German man in the middle of the nineteenth century, and Mrs. Sweet stood still. She loved them both so much, the young Heracles, her husband Mr. Sweet dressed up in the brown corduroy suit which hugged his body so closely, he looked like one of the earliest mammals.

Mrs. Sweet was the mother of the young Heracles and this was as natural and certain as the daily turning of the earth itself. Mrs. Sweet loved the young Heracles, she loved him so and paid special attention to all his needs and indulged him in all his many amusing whims: wanting to see the machines that remove snow—snowplows—at rest in the municipal garage where they were stored when their giant blades were not pushing aside the high drifts of snow. How the young Heracles loved to see that, miles and miles of road covered with snow and the snowplows clearing this away, making a path through it. So too he loved to see tall buildings being assembled with machinery groaning so loudly that he could not hear Mrs. Sweet telling him how much she loved him. And he loved to put on only warm clothes and Mrs. Sweet would cause the sun to shine and make his clothes warm and, if not that, place them in the clothes dryer and warm them up. The young Heracles liked his clothes warm when he put them on and Mrs. Sweet would make them so. But it was the young Heracles who was natural to Mrs. Sweet not the other way around. The young Heracles regarded Mrs. Sweet with disdain and this was correct, for the weak should never be in awe of the strong.

She fretted and worried and became vexed as she thought of his life as he would live it. What if the young Heracles wandered out of the yard in pursuit of one of those balls, be it golf ball, basketball, baseball, football, he playfully and violently made sail through the air? The yard of the Shirley Jackson house had a border. That border was the seasons: winter, spring, summer, and fall. But no matter the season, no matter the weather, the young Heracles played with those balls, Mrs. Sweet mended and knitted those socks, Mr. Sweet lay down on a couch in the dark studio.

The young Heracles now bends down to pick up his shy Myrmidon, a gift he received in his Happy Meal that Mrs. Sweet had bought for him at McDonald's. The shy Myrmidons, tiny figures in blue and green and red plastic, were shy; they clasped their shields to their breasts and held their spears aloft, always ready to strike out and inflict pain, imaginary death. When the young Heracles was four and five and six, he used to line them up against each other on the stairs just outside his room, battlefields, and these plastic figurines would demolish figments, brave figments, over and over again, and then would rest so weary were they from the fighting, and then an unsuspecting and innocent Mr. Sweet would step on their abandoned form and sometimes almost break his neck tumbling down the stairs from that encounter. Oh shit, he would say and then look quickly around, his eyes darting here and there quickly, as if controlled by a mechanical contraption, the little bastard, the little shit. But his mother loved the young Heracles and took him to McDonald's to buy his Happy Meals, even when she was unhappy and did not know that she was so, happiness being the sphere of the young Heracles and his father and her daughter the beautiful Persephone and the shy Myrmidons, made of plastic or not, and any everything else as it came up in the Shirley Jackson house. The young Heracles then bends down to pick up a shy Myrmidon, Then being the same as Now, Then from time to time, becoming Now.

The shy Myrmidons were sometimes lined up, set up in formations, ready to do battle with and triumph over a set of adversaries, whom the young Heracles could not see but neither could the shy Myrmidons and so it all went in this way, a way that would please the young Heracles now, then, then or now, being one and the same burden or pleasure. At other times the shy Myrmidons were separated from each other, scattered here and there, on the floor of the room the young Heracles slept in all by himself; in the bin of the dirty clothes and then rescued from the wash cycle of the washing machine by Mrs. Sweet; on the stairs where Mr. Sweet was walking down just after he got out of bed on a beautiful morning, slipped, and broke his vertebra. The vertebra healed but Mr. Sweet himself did not. The young Heracles said, sorry dad, as he always did, and to say sorry was common to him, as if it were oxygen. Sagging into, sorry dad, and sagging into everything that was now, which would eventually become Then, to all that the young Heracles had strong feelings but the strong feelings would be dealt with then, not now, never now.

But the many shy Myrmidons, the result of many trips to the McDonald's restaurants to purchase many Happy Meals, were lined up and they did go into battle with some imaginary foes and they triumphed of course, again and again, they triumphed of course, and the imaginary battlefield was covered with blood, sheer blood, so much of it, covering everything; so the young Heracles thought, so he said to himself, so he imagined, also. The shy Myrmidons rule, is another thing he said, or imagined. And then he fell asleep. Wake up, wake up, his sister shouted at him, for he did have a sister and she had curly hair. Wake up, his sister shouted at him, a snake with nine heads is lying next to you in your crib. And the very young Heracles then turned over into somersault, and facing the nine-headed snake directly stuck out his tongue at all those heads; without making too much of an effort he tore off their heads and threw them over his shoulder, all nine of them, and they landed on the floor of Mrs. Sweet's newly cleaned kitchen. Oh god, she said to herself, that kid is always up to something, what a mess he has made now. And she picked up the nine snake heads and put them in a bag, wiped up the floor clean, and she asked Mr. Sweet to please come and put out the garbage.

But Mr. Sweet was in his studio above the garage, where he always liked to be, it was not a funeral parlor, it's only that he was in mourning and conducting a funeral for his life, the one he had never led, and Mrs. Sweet's calling him interrupted this mourning, she was always interrupting, his life or his death, she was always interrupting. The studio was dark, then, now, but not completely, everything could be seen clearly but as a shadow of itself. How Mr. Sweet liked that, everything a shadow of itself. But there was that voice of Mrs. Sweet, not the shadow of a voice, she was not capable of that, a whisper, conveying her deepest feelings with a glance, or just stopping her breathing outright, just stop, stop, stop, right now. Mr. Sweet, she would say at the top of her voice, her voice sounding louder than a town crier's, louder than a warning of impending disaster, she was so loud, Mrs. Sweet was so loud. Mr. Sweet, can you please take the garbage out? Sl-aap. Sl-aap, came the sound of his feet that were snug in a pair of flannel slippers as he dragged them across the floor and his rage was so great that it almost brought the now-dead nine-headed snake back to life. In any case his rage was such that it caused his chest to rip open and his heart exploded into pieces but Mrs. Sweet, so used to mending socks, applied her skills to this task and soon had Mr. Sweet all back together, his heart in one piece inside his stitched-back-together chest.

That little jerk almost killed me again, said Mr. Sweet to himself, and it's not the last time, he said again to himself, and he was reminded of that time, not so long ago then, he was coming down the stairs and the young Heracles was going up the same stairs and they met in the middle and by accident collided and by accident the young Heracles, to steady himself from this collision, grabbed Mr. Sweet's entire testicles and threw them away and he threw them with such force that they landed all the way in the Atlantic Ocean, which was Then and is so Now hundreds of miles away. The testicles then fell into that great body of water but did not produce typhoons or tidal waves or hurricanes or volcanic eruptions or unexpected landslides of unbelievable proportions or anything at all noteworthy; they only fell and fell quietly into the deepest part of that body of water and were never heard from again.

Oh, the silence that descended on the household, the Sweet household, as it lived in the Shirley Jackson house: on poor young Heracles, who paused for a very long time at the top of those stairs; on his sister as she curled up in her bed and went to sleep like a single bean seed planted into the rich soil of a treasured vegetable garden; Mr. Sweet removed his fingers from the strings of the lyre; on the dear Mrs. Sweet, who froze over her mending, her knitting, the darning needle in her hand, the knitting needles in her hands just about to pierce the heel of some garment, just about to make complete some garment. And then gathering up herself, surveying what lay in front of her, Mrs. Sweet sorted among the many pairs of socks she had been mending over and over again and removing a pair, she fashioned a new set of organs for her beloved Mr. Sweet, trying and succeeding in making them look identical to the complete set of testicles that had belonged to him and had been destroyed accidentally by his son, the young Heracles. And when Mr. Sweet fell into a sweet sleep of despair after not knowing what to do regarding his lost testicles, Mrs. Sweet sewed the mended socks into their place, the heels of the socks imitating that vulnerable sac of liquid and solid matter that had been Mr. Sweet's testicles.

By then, oh yes then, the beautiful brown hands of the beautiful and dear Mrs. Sweet had turned an un-happy white, all bony and dry. The rest of her remained beautiful brown, a brown that glistened and shone, a brown so unique to her, no other Mrs. Sweet could ever be brown in that way, so glistening, so shiny, so glowing, making her sometimes seem as if she were a secret form of communication, a point of light colliding with the tip of her ear might signify something, might be a signal that enormous changes should be set in motion; or the morning light, briefly coming through the window that was just above the kitchen sink, and for a moment landed on the flat point that was the tip of Mrs. Sweet's flat nose, as she stood there drawing water to make breakfast coffee; the light then would cause such a flash that it could have been taken as a warning against impending cataclysms. But the unhappy whiteness of the bony and dry hands was of no interest to Mrs. Sweet, they blended so well with the worn socks that had to be constantly mended. So Mrs. Sweet went on from then to now and back again.

Then, the time came, out of the blue, when Mr. Sweet fell upon his anger, for he had to face an unavoidable fact, the young Heracles had grown half a foot in one year, and if he did not stop doing that right now he would soon be much bigger than Mr. Sweet. How Mr. Sweet raged quietly in the sunless studio above the garage. To commemorate these feelings, his loneliness, his solitude, his everlasting bereavement, Mr. Sweet wrote a fugue for an orchestra made up of one hundred lyres. "There," he said to Mrs. Sweet presenting to her the score in its entirety, one hundred pages long, "isn't that original, isn't that something no one has ever done before." And Mrs. Sweet, so dear and so sweet she was, knew and so did not have to be told, that she knew nothing at all about music and wondered to herself, where would she find, within the vicinity of the Shirley Jackson house, one hundred musicians who specialized in playing the lyre. The lyre! As she sat at the desk Donald had made for her, a green grasshopper found its way into her sanctuary and she immediately wished it to be a turtle, but it did not become so, and it rubbed its hind legs together, and she winced at the resulting screech. Screech!

The pages and pages of the score for Mr. Sweet's fugue were so heavy they caused Mrs. Sweet to bend over under their weight. What to do? What should she do? Mrs. Sweet scoured the surrounding area of villages and hamlets, looking inside their churches and synagogues and homeless shelters, and then sought advice from heads of households and homeless wanderers until, after years and years, she gathered together one hundred distinguished musicians who specialized in playing the lyre. They assembled and made a crowd on the small green area that was just off the house in which Shirley Jackson had lived for a time. But then Mr. Sweet came down with a cold and also his shoulders froze and his throat was red and sore and his feet fell flat and a great fear of open spaces overcame him.

The shy Myrmidons were lined up side by side, their plastic yellow hair flowing in the same direction as their plastic green tunics, away from their bodies, giving them a look of never-ending and prompt motion. Across from them were the legions of plastic men wearing turtle shells and bearing swords ready to strike the shy Myrmidons. The young Heracles had gotten the legions of plastic men who wore turtle shells and carried swords as a bonus with his Happy Meals too and again he never ate the meals themselves, only he so liked the things that came with them: shy Myrmidons, men wearing turtle shells, or sometimes a cape draped over their shoulders, horses with wings, birds with men's feet. The shy Myrmidons now attacked the legions of men wearing the turtle shell and there was blood everywhere mixed up with bones and shell and other kinds of bodily matter, and amid all the imaginary cries and shrieks of imaginary suffering, there was the sound of Mr. Sweet revising and rewriting parts of his fugue, the sweet notes becoming bitter, the bitter notes becoming more so. Standing high above the blood, the bones, and the other kinds of bodily matter (for he was so tall, the young Heracles), the young Heracles spun around on the ball of one foot, the other foot perfectly crooked in midair to lend him balance, and he laughed a big and loud laugh that rippled all across the valley and came to a stop on the side of the mountain that rose above this same valley and came back toward the young Heracles and his home in the old Shirley Jackson house but not before touching down lightly on the Jewish graveyard where his ancient ancestors were buried and the golf course and Powers Market and the Paper Mill Bridge.

Heracles, Heracles, said Mrs. Sweet to herself, but though no one else could hear this, to her the sound of his name then was as if she were in a small room with all sensation shut out, only the name, Heracles, filling up that time then and that space now. Often, the name of her son left her with such a sensation, his name and so he himself, took up, filled up everything, time or space, space or time, one or the other. For Mrs. Sweet, his name then caused the shallow furrow in her brow to deepen but this deepening could only be seen with the help of a microscope. And Mr. Sweet, on hearing this big and loud laugh, wished his son a safe passage to the edge of the universe in a faulty space capsule; how he would like to see the look on the young Heracles' face after an event like that.

But then: one hundred lyres, one hundred musicians to play them, thought Mrs. Sweet and she went about her duties, making the instruments and the musicians. Her concentration was unwavering, her devotion was without question, her love had no limits. How the dear Mrs. Sweet loved Mr. Sweet and so too she loved all that he produced, fugues, concertos, choral pieces, suites, and variations. But the one million lyres and musicians to play them! Mrs. Sweet set about her task. She planted field upon field of cotton and sugarcane and indigo and dispatched many families to the salt mines. Mrs. Sweet brought her produce to market as cash crops, as manufactured goods, as raw human labor, and made an outlandish profit and with her profit she then made lyres and people who could play them and then she built a concert hall, a concert hall so large that to experience it required the fanaticism of a pilgrim. On that day when Mrs. Sweet gathered the lyres and the people who could play them in the great concert hall in which that elaborate and complicated and unique and earth-changing fugue of Mr. Sweet's was to be finally played, Mr. Sweet came down with a case of sore tendons in his heels. And it was very true, his heels were sore they hurt so much, and on top of that what rage came over him to see that the dear Mrs. Sweet had made his impossible demand possible. In this atmosphere of Mrs. Sweet's accomplishments, so magical they were, Mr. Sweet grew, but in resentment and hatred, not in love, not in gratitude.

I have not lived my life as a scholar, said Mr. Sweet, still smarting from the insults Mrs. Sweet had hurled at him, especially that recent one with the concert hall and the one hundred musicians; she had asked him to close the garage door behind him, wash the dishes, wipe down the counter, clean the kitchen sink, take out the garbage, I have not lived my life as a scholar it is true, said Mr. Sweet, but neither was I meant to do such things, I cannot do such things.

And Mr. Sweet lay down on the chair in his studio above the garage, the chair with legs that ended in the shape of the paws of a large cat. A loud crack and a roar came through the closed windows. The young Heracles had released his pride of caged lions. A current of hatred traveled quickly through Mr. Sweet's body but it did not threaten to consume him, and so he settled down and looked up. Above him was the domed ceiling painted a cerulean blue, receding into infinity if looked at unblinkingly for too long. Dim lights appeared here and there, and then brightly shone the constellations starting with Orion, Ursa Major, Ursa Minor, the Big Dipper, the Little Dipper, arc to Arcturus, Canis Major and Minor, Castor and Pollux, and on and on expanding ever outward to the edge of night. Pyramids of thoughts and feelings hounded the dear man now as he lay sweetly on the chair: his beloved flannel-covered slippers that had been given to him by his mother when he turned twelve years old had developed holes in their soles and the slippers could not be repaired and they could not be replaced exactly, for no longer were slippers of that kind made. Mr. Sweet could still wear those slippers even now that he was a middle-aged man, he had not grown a half inch since he turned twelve. The world was cold and unmindful of his poor soul. The sky above, even as it was just the cerulean-blue ceiling in the studio above the garage, was vast, and it expanded out, smooth and also rippling, containing heavens and havens too, spaces that pulsed like an important artery in a body but without its importance or responsibility, spaces in which everyday experience could not settle. The thin edge of night, not so dark yet, framed the cerulean blue. The thin edge of night will give way to an unyielding darkness but Mr. Sweet just then held this, the thin edge of night, not too close to him. The thin edge of night is a metaphor, I shall write a symphony, a covert allusion to this, the thin edge of night is a metaphor, said Mr. Sweet to himself, and only to himself. In the meantime, the fixed point in the cerulean-blue ceiling expanded and expanded in Mr. Sweet's mind, as if he had been influenced by a consciousness-altering drug or as if he had willed himself to see it so. The universe, or so it seemed to Mr. Sweet or anyone else and by anyone else he meant Mrs. Sweet, the young Heracles, and the sister with the lustrous curls, as he lay face upward; the thin edge of night expanded outward and outward and descended on him and then swallowed him up and in it he slept and slept and slept and slept!

The battalion of shy Myrmidons was scattered across the lawn and in Mrs. Sweet's flower beds, some of them lying face down, some of them lying faceup. The young Heracles stood above them, a fallen branch, dead at that, of the hemlock in his right hand. Whooo! Yeaah! Aaargh! Eeee-agh! A series of sounds escaped from him, sometimes angry, sometimes not. He bent down and arranged the battalion of shy Myrmidons. Some of them were missing; some of them had become entangled in the roots of Mrs. Sweet's hibiscus causing the roots to girdle, growing around and around, viciously entangling themselves and this would end in their death. But the dear and sweet young Heracles did not know that, how could he, Mrs. Sweet was his mother, his mother was Mr. Sweet's wife, Mr. Sweet was his father, the young Heracles was Mr. Sweet's son. The dear son of Mr. Sweet looked down on his battalion of shy Myrmidons, they all lay at his feet and some of them had become entangled in the roots of the hibiscus variety "Lord Baltimore," variety "Anne Arundel," variety "Lady Baltimore," all of which were growing in Mrs. Sweet's garden. Ants crawled all over the shy Myrmidons as they went about their ant business; bees flew in and then flew out of the pollen-laden blossoms of the hibiscus in Mrs. Sweet's garden, and a hummingbird did this too. And the young Heracles gathered up the shy Myrmidons and placed them in a large black box, and set them aside for a while, a long while.

3

At dusk one day, the young Heracles was born, and Mr. Sweet, who then appeared to be as tall as a young prince in Tudor times, smiled at his son and kissed his cheeks, and then he cut his young son's umbilical cord. He looked at the newborn boy and was afraid to hold him close because he had the strongest desire to drop him out of his arms, see him fall to the ground, his body intact except for his head, his brains scattered all over the floor of the delivery room that was in the hospital in the town that was not so far away from the Shirley Jackson house. Mrs. Sweet, lying on the bed, her legs wide open, still in the position she had been when the young Heracles came out of her womb, her womb it is from which the young Heracles emerged, her whole body shivering from the effort of bringing Mr. Sweet's son into the world, she looked at them, her old husband, her new son, and fell asleep from weariness. "How to secure my kingdom, so that I can give to, leave an inheritance for the young Heracles, who is my only son, so far?" was not what

Mr. Sweet thought to himself at all, at all, not at all. He so hated the young Heracles, just born and new and yellow was the color of his skin, for he had jaundice, and his eyes were open wide and they looked as if they saw everything even though everything could not yet be understood. Such eyes, such eyes, said Mr. Sweet to himself, such eyes, they would never see and so lead to an understanding of Beethoven's concertos and Mozart and Bach, and in any case the young Heracles had hands that were big, suggesting a clumsiness to come, for such hands would never hold a lyre comfortably if at all or linger over a pianoforte or hold a flute to the lips or hold any instruments to the lips or caress any instruments at all; his fingers were big as if meant to hold a javelin and a shield and to tear to shreds things many times his size. So thought Mr. Sweet as he held his son in his arms, his hands, his own fingers were delicate and looked as if they were musical notes rising up and floating freely above empty sheets of notepaper and then landing in an order that resulted in the most beautiful tunes especially when whistled. But Mr. Sweet did not throw to the ground or let fall out of his hands the young Heracles, and so their story continued, with a bitterness for Mr. Sweet that had a taste familiar to the tongue and with a bitterness that had a taste familiar to the ages; the ages and ages of fathers who did not love their sons.

•

But he cut the umbilical cord of the young Heracles, that lifeline all human beings have to their mothers, and this is always an honorable and loving thing to do, and the newly born baby Heracles had jaundice and this made his mother nervous for she loved him so immediately she saw him. She loved his eyes, those very ones that were so wide and looked as if he could see everything that they did not understand, his past was his future and he could see it, even though he didn't understand it; anyway, she loved her little son and was sorry to see him lying, stark naked, in a hospital bassinet, under some lights, his yellow skin getting more so until he looked almost like a marigold, so she thought, and she grew more worried as she held him to her breasts, two large sacks full of milk, and she held him so tight he almost melted into her, but he did not; instead he grew well, eventually getting rid of the jaundice condition, for it was caused by her blood type being at odds with Mr. Sweet's blood type as it pumped its way around and inside the little body of the young Heracles. This condition lasted seven days and on the eighth day he was released from the hospital and sent home with his parents, Mr. and Mrs. Sweet, who lived in the Shirley Jackson house. It was not a day in September, it was a day in another month, the month of June, and peonies were in bloom, some special ones, white petals with a single streak of red randomly appearing on each petal; and irises too and columbine and a rose named Stanley Perpetual.

Outside the house, there was a large old silver maple tree, as there would be outside a house such as the Shirley Jackson house, and it had old wounds here and there from the many times it had been struck by lightning. Outside too was an old apple tree, so diseased it hardly could muster any blooms and so was never with fruit; and also there was a pear tree and it did bear fruit but it was bitter and could never be eaten. The grass was green and just starting to grow rampantly, waiting for the first mowing. Aaaaaaaah! That was a sound that came from inside the house, a sigh of exquisite satisfaction, and it was made by Mrs. Sweet. She was standing over the baby, her son, looking down at him as he lay propped up on his side, one little arm underneath one little cheek, the other little arm curled up and resting under his chin, his skin the color of a healthy baby. His eyes were closed.

•

Oh, the lovely, lovely baby, so thought Mrs. Sweet and she gazed down at her sweet son, lying in his cradle, on top of sheets she had made herself just for him, and he was wearing one of the many little tunics she had knitted for him, taking instructions from a book entitled *The Right Way to Knit*; she had bought that book at the North-shire bookstore, in a town not far away from the village in which she lived with her family, a happy existence with her family, especially now with the addition of the young Heracles. The boy, just lying there, his chest moving up and down ever so imperceptibly, his young heart, his young life, just beginning: what will his destiny be, thought his mother, what cruel surprises will life hold for him, what unfair labors await him, what harsh tasks he will overcome, yes, he will triumph over them, thought his wonderful mother, who had taught herself knitting from a book and had taught herself to cook meals eaten in the many different regions of France from a book, who had taught herself how to make a garden from a book, who had taught herself how to be, but that was from instinct, not a book. And she loved her little son, the baby, as if he were a firstborn but he was not, she loved her firstborn in just the same way she loved the young Heracles, her firstborn, a girl, that was the beautiful Persephone, but Mr. Sweet kept the beautiful Persephone away from her mother, because in his mind Mrs. Sweet was so much of another world, a world of goods—people included—that came on ships; he kept her to himself in the studio, for it was very important that she stay near his lyre, she was such an inspiration to him, he wrote hymns for her to sing and other music suitable for voice, just for her, and the beautiful Persephone sang them extremely well, worthy of a theater but Mr. Sweet would not allow anyone else to hear her, and if by some accident they did hear her he discouraged them from thinking her voice beautiful, for they might take her away, far from the space above the garage in the Shirley Jackson house and Mr. Sweet would be all alone and he would die and he was afraid to die, even though he already was.

But . . . Mrs. Sweet so loved the young Heracles and to gaze down on him forever was one of her "one desires." He was so beautiful but not in comparison to anything else, he was so beautiful and most beautiful all by himself. He had thick hairs growing just above his eyes and this made him look like a lion; but then he had enormous round eyes (they were closed now in sleep, as Mrs. Sweet looked down on him) and this made him look like an owl; but then he had a very broad nose, which made him look like an imagined bear, a teddy bear, a toy meant to calm children; his mouth, oh his mouth was as wide as the sun's, that very sun that rises up above the known-by-all horizon and then covers the sky for a while, a while being a day, and to witness this event, the sun rising up from the horizon and covering the expanse of sky for the time it does, is a very definition of being alive; his ears were huge, the lobes themselves looking like a peculiar kind of flower that is found in a unique ecosystem and also like a satellite dish, an instrument made to receive information in a way not common to other human beings. As Mrs. Sweet was standing over him, admiring his baby form, his young tenderness, and seeing in his glorious features outstanding attributes, she wept, the tears flowing uncontrollably and in such volume, that she had to immediately gather them up and place them outside, making a pond, in which frogs, trout, and the like would live and lay their eggs. Oh, she said to herself, oh, his beauty will drown me, it is so much like the force of something immortal: the river in Mahaut, Dominica, that her mother had to cross each day on her way to school; the tree-clad mountains, that sometimes were a glittering green with new leaves and sometimes a blinding gold with old leaves, to be seen from any vantage, inside or outside, of the Shirley Jackson house; the moon, as it is portrayed and seen in a book called *Goodnight Moon* that she used to read to her first great love, the everlasting, deeply harmonious, beautiful Persephone.

•

The telephone rang; Mrs. Sweet's entire being shook; her body of course but her presence of mind, too. Who could it be: the bill collectors; the telephone company named Verizon; the cable TV provider called something else; Blue Flame, a natural-gas company that supplied energy for cooking food and making the water hot for a bath, if the Sweets wished for such a thing; oil for heating the house; an angry voice demanding payment for the car loans; Paul, who cleans the chimneys; Mr. Pembroke, who cleans the yard; the Haydens, father and son, who have stopped the two bathroom pipes from leaking into the kitchen; a friend of the Sweets wanting to wish them good luck with the arrival of the young Heracles; a friend of the Sweets who has a special feeling of friendship for Mr. Sweet, not a love affair of steamy sex, just a friend who does not like Mrs. Sweet, who prefers Mr. Sweet; a friend who thought it would be a fine thing if Mrs. Sweet could be thrown from a great height and not die, from this fall, only becoming a cripple afterwards.

The telephone rang: Mrs. Sweet thought, oh what is that and who is it? And Mr. Sweet said, I'll get it, for he had heard that sound, it mingled in with the sharp and flat notes. On his way to the phone he could see the young Heracles lying inside his little crib and his mother had been standing over him in a fit of imagining his future, remembering his future too, for the fate of a child is in the memory of the mother! The boy hero was asleep in his crib, on sheets made by Mrs. Sweet with her own hands, he could remember the nights in dark winter, when she should have been listening to his compositions of fugues and other somber tunes, she was knitting away, knitting away, weaving blankets, weaving sheets and diapers too, knitting tunics and such, and it was very disrespectful, for the creation of a thing is superior to the creation of a person, so thought Mr. Sweet to himself! That boy and his mother would become a title for a song to be sung by children, thought Mr. Sweet, and he made a mental note of that: Mrs. Sweet adoring her son and imagining her son's greatness in the world that was to come, his triumphs, for here he is shooting the basketball in the hoop, when the hoop itself was miles away, and the golf ball into the hole when the hole itself was miles away, and hitting the baseball way out of the boundaries of the baseball park; and the baseball park itself was as big as the seventeenth largest island on the surface of the earth. Mrs. Sweet imagined her son's future and they were very bitter images to Mr. Sweet. Seeing this scene of the adoring mother worshipping her young son, a hero to her already, as he lay sleeping in his little crib, how Mr. Sweet hated Mrs. Sweet and his hatred for the young Heracles, new to him, its reality new to him, increased; but this hatred was a new form of discomfort, so Mr. Sweet thought to himself. All the same, Mr. Sweet hated the young boy and wished that a family of snakes would appear from nowhere and devour him! But that did not become so, just then or ever. And so Mr. Sweet, sulking away, though that is too tame a word to describe his disturbance, his hatred, his confusion, thought of a number of dishes he could serve to Mrs. Sweet, if only he could cook: a soufflé of a young baby with no name; poached new baby with no name; a saddle of the young Heracles with lemon and thyme; she would devour them, for she loved to eat, anyone could see it in her expanding waist, the thickening of her upper arms, her eyelids, the lobes of her ears, her ankles like the feet of chairs in the drawing rooms of well-off people, meant to represent well-loved and domesticated animals; oh how Mr. Sweet hated Mrs. Sweet: she looked like something to eat, but afterwards you would hate even the thought of eating; and he could see her stout, overly well-fed body dead, in the hills of Montana or Vermont or somewhere like that, you know, where the leaves are turning gold, yellow, red because they are about to drop to the ground and become a metaphor, and metaphors are the true realm of a creator. But just then, as if she were seeing now, as clearly as she was in the present, Mrs. Sweet had a memory of her old friend Matt, who was the manageress of a grocery store that sold special cheeses and special hams and special yogurts and special everything necessary to cook a good meal from a cookbook written by Marcella Hazan or Paula Peck or Elizabeth David. And Matt, who lived with someone named Dan or Jim, Mrs. Sweet could not remember his name exactly right then, only that he spoke brilliantly about the weather, about the atmosphere, naturally, physically in which we would all live Then, and Now too. Matt gave Mrs. Sweet a number of recipes for cornbread: Edna Lewis, a cook whose family had its origins in slave society in Virginia; Nika Hazelton, whose recipe for cornbread Matt had adapted so that Mrs. Sweet had no interest in the original, for she loved Matt not in just that way she loved Mr. Sweet or the young Heracles; but her love for Matt was an exception, Mrs. Sweet loved her friend. But can love, all by itself, in isolation, be understood, or trusted even?

But the telephone did ring and Mr. Sweet answered it and it was someone from a utilities company—one of the many in the now-known world—someone from a company who supplied an essential component that kept the Sweet household a reasonably comfortable place in which to find yourself. Mr. Sweet gave reassuring answers, explaining the delays of payment in a way that never brought up the truth that the Sweets could not at that moment pay their bills, and he did it with such conviction and in any case what he was saying was believed, and this convincing falseness made him feel that he had gotten away with murder; not the murder of Mrs. Sweet or the young Heracles, because he only wished to kill them, not murder them.

And so that passed in the moment, the Sweets, Mr. and Mrs., with their respective positions regarding their young son, from very different perspectives, as the boy lay in his crib, clad in his little tunic that had been wrought with loving purpose by Mrs. Sweet, his tunic that was a shield from the natural elements from which a newborn child must be protected. But Mr. Sweet was much vexed, for bills and such everyday matters interfered with how he thought the world, you know, the everyday, should progress: for instance, when you, or anyone for that matter, turn on the light switch, the light, be it in the ceiling or a lamp on a table, will come on; when he wanted hot water for his coffee (he liked instant coffee, Maxwell House) he had only to turn on the stove and a brilliant flame would appear and make the water hot and then he would have his beverage and this is how he began each day; when he wanted to call his mother and father, who were at that time in the grave, he picked up the phone and dialed: who should pay for it all, who should pay for living itself, this was a question that so concerned Mrs. Sweet and why did Mr. Sweet not know her, not know who she really was, not know she was a virus, the cold that brought you low in summer.

I hate her, thought Mr. Sweet, but she billowed toward him, in a long white nightgown she had bought from the Laura Ashley store on Fifty-seventh Street between Fifth and Madison Avenues in New York City; the cost of this garment could have paid for a month's worth of telephone calls to her relatives who lived far away, or a day's worth of drugs that could keep a person who was dying of AIDS alive for weeks then, or the fee of the copyists who copied the complicated jumble of notes that Mr. Sweet said was music. That nightgown, so light in fabric, for it was woven from cotton grown in Egypt, so romantic in the imagination of the person who made it and who later died after falling down some stairs, could so easily be transformed into a noose, but how to get Mrs. Sweet to put her neck into it? Mr. Sweet came into the room, looked down at the baby Heracles, and kissed his wife. See Now Then, See Then Now, just to see anything at all, especially the present, was to always be inside the great world of disaster, catastrophe, and also joy and happiness, but these two latter are not accounted for in history, they were and are relegated to personal memory. And she looked at her son again lying in his baby bed and in no particular order and also all at once these thoughts and accompanying feelings overwhelmed her. The episiotomy, a necessary wound made by the doctor (Barbara was her name) in charge of the safe delivery of the young Heracles, caused Mrs. Sweet much pain, a pain that she had not imagined ever, but should have had a memory of it because that same gash had been made in her vagina when she was giving birth to the boy's sister, but this kind of pain, this particular kind of pain, another person living comfortably inside you and then, after a while, forcing themselves out into the world, and in doing so tears apart your body, and you will love them more than anybody else will love them, such pain, so much of it, and sometimes it had a texture, rough, undulating, sharp, and stinging, intermittent, then flat and cold and constant.

The curtains were drawn and yet through them Mrs. Sweet could see that the light in the Yellow House, a house painted a yellow so clear and untinged with any other colors, a color yellow that Mrs. Sweet had once seen in Finland and Estonia, places not at all near the equator; in the Yellow House lived a family, a mother, a father, and six children and all those six children were so wonderfully well adjusted to life as it was, so well behaved, so polite, so kind (there were four girls and two boys and the boys have never been known to drown a hamster just to see what that would be like or cut off a cat's whiskers and then let him be alone in the woods to see what that would be like), that Mrs. Sweet wished that her family—Mr. Sweet, the beautiful Persephone, the young Heracles—would be just like the children of the family who lived in the Yellow House and their name was Blue: Mr. and Mrs. Benjamin Blue. Until she was thirteen years of age Mrs. Sweet wet her bed every night while she was asleep and it made her afraid to fall asleep even until now, this now, and it is why she counts an imaginary flock of sheep as she tries to fall asleep each night and fails and so swallows a capsule of Restoril. Every Halloween Mr. Blue transformed himself into a very attractive woman, his legs free of hair and his underarms too, and that could be seen, for he wore panty hose and a dramatically sleeveless dress; and he wore a pair of shoes with very high heels, heels so high they made Mrs. Sweet laugh, she thought shoes in that shape were a form of amusement, that even when women wore them they were meant to make everybody who saw them laugh, not outright, not to themselves a secret, not altogether, only just say to themselves, here is a laugh. But that was Mr. Blue, every Halloween, wearing a costume of a dress and a beautiful wig and earrings and bracelets and false pearls and stockings (fishnet sometimes, sheer flesh-colored or not sometimes); and sometimes when Mrs. Sweet saw him, for it happened year after year, a long time, and this time, year after year, a long time is five years, which to Mrs. Sweet was a forever; she said to herself: How does he do it? What does his wife think? Are his children, all six of them, four girls, two boys, pleased to see their father, so unusual in our small world confined and defined by the presence of the Shirley Jackson house, looking more like a beautiful woman than most beautiful women can manage, and asking of us all to find nothing in it except delight, delight, and more delight? And, each year after Mr. Blue and Mr. Sweet had done taking the children trick-or-treating, Mrs. Sweet would sit with Mr. Blue at the dining-room table and they would drink Cavalier rum from small glass tumblers.

Every morning is the next morning of the night before: and the night before is Now and Then at the same time is the morning after the night before: the young Heracles crying loudly, as if he meant to wake up the whole world, and Mrs. Sweet had to give him milk from those sacs attached to her chest and he drank from her as if he were the earth itself on which rain had not fallen for three or seven or ten years.

And all that while during the time of the birth and then infancy of the young Heracles Mr. Sweet had fallen asleep, ignoring his wife in her beautiful night-gown, sleeping through the faint cries of the baby, though any passerby might perceive this cry as coming from the throat of an army of murderous men, who meant to kill or be killed, he slept peaceably, in contentment, in a state of sleep that any scientist who has studied sleep would declare ideal, perfect, a state of sleep to be universally prescribed. And he slept through the nights, satisfied completely in the world of sleep, dreaming of a universe in which every conscious being was a triumph and all that they imagined themselves to be was all they would be; and there was harmony in matters of every kind: physical, emotional, mental; and in such a universe, Mrs. Sweet loved her husband so much until the end of time and time would never end. Next to her was his body, the size of a young Tudor prince, buried beneath white cotton sheets purchased from somewhere and a blanket and a duvet, all draped over him in such a way, he looked like a living and breathing sacred relic, a sarcophagus, lost to her world, the world in which she lived in the Shirley Jackson house and beyond, lost to the Blues, and the Elwells, and the Jennings, whose mentally unstable son drowned their dog in urine he had collected from many sources, and the Pembrokes sending their workers to mow the lawn; and the Atlases, who lived in a house near the Walloom-sac River; and the Woolmingtons, whom Mrs. Sweet loved, for just their sheer existence made her life a joy; the Josephs, who went hunting each hunting season and would return with a shot-dead deer and then after re-moving its skin would hang it up on the door of the barn, a display for communal adoration; and this scene of deer hunting admitted Homer Now and Then, then there were the two old ladies who sold newspapers, or so they said, but also sold a collection of magazines, with varying titles, devoted to motorbikes, and the illustrations to accompany the articles were many pictures of naked women, posed in positions that would make anyone want to have sex with them; and then there were the oth-ers, families who experienced happiness and despair, but right then, just then. At dawn Mrs. Sweet was up, out of bed, and looking around her and seeing nothing really, or seeing the bed in which she lay, her husband next to her, the sun about to pour too much of itself into the day, no cries of hunger or any other deep, essential need came from the newborn Heracles, the birds were singing, the bats, whose graceful sweepings about in the unknown and so therefore matterless air frightened Mrs. Sweet, were returning to wherever they concealed themselves during the day; a rumble from the engines of cars with passengers going to some destination that made up the world in which the Sweets and their acquaintances, or people they depended on, was very loud and then flew by like the sound coming from a wind instrument that was so elaborate, its base rested on the floor and the person playing it had to sit on a sturdy chair; Mrs. Sweet wanted to make a cup of coffee, but had been warned that an essential ingredient of that delicious beverage could harm a newborn's development if it turned up in her breast milk, and so she made herself a cup of tea from fresh mint leaves she had gathered from an ineradicable patch of mint and let it steep in the water heated in a fragile electric water-heating pot she and Mr. Sweet had bought at KMart, and drank the tea when she felt it was good to do so.

Oh, what a morning it was, that first morning of Mrs. Sweet awaking before the baby Heracles with his angry cries, declaring his hunger, the discomfort of his wet diaper, the very aggravation of being new and in the world; the rays of sun were falling on the just and the unjust, the beautiful and the ugly, causing the innocent dew to evaporate; the sun, the dew, the little waterfall right next to the village's firehouse, making a roar, though really it was an imitation of the roar of a real waterfall; the smell of some flower, faint, as it unfurled its petals for the first time: oh what a morning! A time for reflection, for remembering the past, that way of seeing Then Now: an afternoon in winter, the middle of February, and Mrs. Sweet was not Mrs. Sweet yet, though she and Mr. Sweet were married by then, she was still young and had a personality that was not yet Mrs. Sweet; she wore strange clothes, dresses that were fashionable years ago among housewives who lived in that area called the Great Plains and that they had made themselves from patterns they ordered and received through the post office. Mrs. Sweet would find these garments in stores named Enid's, Harriet Love, stores that sold old clothes that were fashionable long ago, and other things too: a lamp, a chair, a desk, her typewriter, drinking-water glasses and coffee cups, cast-iron pots, a table with a top made of thickly layered white enamel that had been baked, and many other things, all useful and all had been used by other people who had been alive not so long ago, these things were secondhand, or thirdhand, numerous unknown hands had claimed them before— yes, all that Mrs. Sweet lived with in her Then, had a Then before her; now, she smiled, not to herself, she smiled openly, her fat and wide lips spreading across her face, and to see it would be to see a definition of gladness or a picture of happiness or a person enjoying herself completely; and an afternoon in a winter that had appeared unexpectedly to Mrs. Sweet in the early morning—Then, Now—made her remember the color of the sun's light, as it shone down on the concrete walls of an empty building which she could see while sitting at her used desk, in her used chair, in front of the used typewriter and trying to see a Then—because there is always a Then to see Now—the light was a soft mauve (though she thought of mauve as a soft purple), like a semi-precious stone (amethyst), like a field of lavender (*L. officinalis*) that had not been harvested . . . and at the time, then, Mrs. Sweet dissolved in a sweet sadness, for she could not find any more similes for this light that fell on the wall of the empty building and she sat down and wrote a short story about her childhood and it took up no more than three pages, for just then she could only bear the memory of her childhood for that amount of time and space.

But that morning was just the beginning of that day, and after watching the whizzing by to their purposeful destinations of many of the people who made her life run smoothly (not less difficult), and after experiencing a moment of Then, Now (the memory of being young and living in New York, at 284 Hudson Street, just married to Mr. Sweet, being in love with him, and everything that he knew, because he so well understood the many theories, the theories that made up her Now). And then the adorable, shrieking, panic-causing, irritating cry of the young Heracles reached her ears, not in a winding motion but like the strike of a thunderbolt sent from a god, then came Mr. Sweet and he asked if she could make his breakfast of toast Chernobyl (he liked his toast burnt), a bowl of Cheerios with canned peaches, and a cup of instant Maxwell House coffee with cream-less milk. The baby, said Mrs. Sweet to Mr. Sweet. The baby? he answered, and then he said, oh yes, poor young Heracles, I had a dream about him last night, and Mrs. Sweet fled to the upstairs of the Shirley Jackson house and found the room in which lay the young Heracles in his little crib, and she picked him up and brought him to her bosom, where the overflowing sacs of milk sat. He drank from them with a ferociousness only possible in a fable, he drank from them as if the future of some great but not-yet-known civilization depended on this act, he drank as if he knew there was a Then and a Now, and a Now from which a Then could would come, time being completely beyond human understanding. And Mrs. Sweet was drained, exhausted, depleted, but how she loved the young Heracles as she looked down on him and he did not know that his life depended on her.

4

Hail the young Heracles, said Mrs. Sweet to herself and then repeated it in a whisper in the ears of her precious son (for he was that, her precious son), and she took him in her arms and kissed him and then tossed him up in the air and caught him firmly and held him aloft and looked into his eyes and they laughed in each other's face. In his eyes then Mrs. Sweet could see her own self reflected: she was almost as big as an average-sized garden shed, so she told herself, though Mr. Sweet had said to her that she looked like the actor Charles Laughton when he portrayed the captain of a ship, sailing from the South Pacific with a cargo of saplings, in which the crew mutinied. Mrs. Sweet knew the movie very well, for the cargo of the ship at the time the crew mutinied was the bread-fruit, a staple of Mrs. Sweet's diet when she had been a child, and it had been a staple of the diet of children born for generations before hers and all of those children hated this food. Then, when she was a child, she was very thin and her mother, she did not have a father, worried very much about her. Her mother, believing that the un-cooked liver of cows would make the child Mrs. Sweet strong, sought this out from a butcher she had made friends with at the meat market; her mother grated car-rots with a grater made by an old Portuguese man, a man who made things like that, and also soldered old tin cans for their household use: cups, pots, shit pots, things like that; and squeezed the juice out of the grated carrots and made the little girl, who was not yet Mrs. Sweet, drink it. And so, when Mr. Sweet compared her bodily form, after the birth of the young Heracles, to the cap-tain of that awful ship, Mrs. Sweet almost wept, but then, Mr. Sweet laughed at this comment he had made, he often thought he had just said the funniest thing that was ever said in all the history of funny things said, when right then and now, he had not.

But not really minding any of that then, which was right now, for Now will be Then and Then is right at this very moment: Mrs. Sweet held the young Hera-cles close to her and kissed the top of his head and then his cheeks and his mouth and his eyes (when he saw her lips move closer that way, he closed them) and his ears and then his baby-fat little chin and neck and then his chest and then she buried her full face into his stomach and with her mouth made sounds that might be like a fart or a pig squealing in torment or a clown laughing in a way that would frighten the children she had been hired to entertain. But the young Heracles loved all of it, kisses and sounds and in particular he loved the smell of his mother, for to him she neither looked like nor smelled like a captain of anything; he loved her face as it hovered over him: the eyes black, dark as a night that had yet to be invented, black as if waiting to give a meaning to light, so black it made light itself disappear forever; the nose like the nose of a water-dwelling mammal; the cheeks like the top of a bun; and the lips and mouth, so big, as if together they were keeping in check an unknown geographical expanse. That was Mrs. Sweet's face as it appeared to the young Heracles, still a baby, not yet being able to walk, just being able to sit up on his own without being surrounded and propped up with pillows and cushions and sometimes his mother's large body, that was her face as it hovered above, and at times, as she held him aloft, as he hovered over her. And he called his mother Mrs. Sweet, for she appeared to him to be so sweet, as if she were something to eat, and then he called her Mom, knowing without knowing that he had once drunk milk from her breast, his only food then, his sole source of nourishment.

The young Heracles went through the stages of crawling, though he was very awkward at it, and at trying to pull himself up from a sitting position, and after many tries, he one day could do this; and then not long after, he could walk across the room by himself, though at that time, Then, he did not walk in the way walking is known to be, instead, he projected himself across the room in which he stood, from one side to the other and when successfully reaching the opposite place from where he started out would burst out in laughter and clap his hands in happiness, so proud was he of his own accomplishment. Mrs. Sweet shared his joy, how could she not, she loved him so! When one day Mr. Sweet observed this performance, he later asked Mrs. Sweet if perhaps the young Heracles should not see a specialist, for the way he hurled himself across the room seemed abnormal. Mrs. Sweet said, hmmmmmh! and then chewed her nails down to the quick, how to pay the enormous heating bill from Greene's Oil and the electric-light bill from Central Vermont Public Service. For how were they to live? Mrs. Sweet asked herself and then she looked up at the heavens and from time to time a large check would fall out of the clear blue sky and it was addressed to her; and then again, from time to time, the postman would bring lots of sealed envelopes and when the envelopes were addressed to Mrs. Sweet, inevitably they held checks made payable to that Charles Laughton–like entity. Mr. Sweet would look up at the sky too and see out of its true blueness the white envelopes falling down to the earth, and all the envelopes were addressed to Mrs. Sweet; Mr. Sweet would intercept the postman just as he was about to deposit all the Sweets' mail in their mailbox and all the envelopes were addressed to Mrs. Sweet and some of them held checks made out to Mrs. Sweet. Here, it's all for you, Mr. Sweet would say, throwing the contents of the mail on the dining table, not caring how it landed, in what order it appeared, and to himself, he would say, "She is such a shit," but Mrs. Sweet would never hear it, for he said it to himself, he said so many things to himself and only he, only he, heard himself say these things.

•

The young Heracles soon could walk in a normal way, one foot, not parallel, in front of the other, each allowing him to balance himself, and he did so with great peals of laughter and other exclamations of joy! And he went from one room to the other without inhibition, and in his joy at this he would shout, "I did it, I did it," and this declaration of his accomplishment was a source of intrigue to Mrs. Sweet, for what did it mean, "I did it, I did it," and the triumph of the young Heracles, for he broke free of the borders between the kitchen and the dining room and the living room and the doors that led to outside, where there would be a road with cars going back and forth to unknown destinations and their drivers heedless of the occasional presence of the young Heracles; this triumph of the young Heracles was such a mystery to Mrs. Sweet. But Mr. Sweet looked at the damage done when that small child, no more than a year old, went from room to room, in his herolike struggle, his strong body shoving the furniture out the window, tearing down the curtains and shredding them into pieces as if they were tissue paper, throwing up his half-digested vegetables all over the white couch for the fun of it: and he thought, what the hell is this! what is the matter with this kid! where the hell did he come from! For that boy, the young Heracles, could die if he was not contained in the rooms of the Shirley Jackson house, with its yard separating it from the busy street, and Mr. Sweet did not desire this: that the young Heracles be struck dead by a car driven by someone drunk or driven by a teenager as the young Heracles in exhilaration wandered out into the nice country road, without being noticed by his dear mother, that loving Mrs. Sweet, he had not desired at all. And so Mr. Sweet went to Ames, a department store that then sold many useful things at a price the Sweets could afford, and he bought many sets of safety guards, expandable barriers, which when placed between two doorposts blocked entry from one room to the other, and he also bought locks for the cabinets that held dangerous substances, in the kitchen, bathroom and other appropriate places, and these locks were so complicated that only an adult person could manage to unlock them. But here comes the young Heracles! For his fingers so thick and ungainly-seeming were so intelligent they knew how to unlock the cabinets that held the poisonous liquids that a child might swallow and he was so strong that when he, in a fit of running, threw himself against the child-barrier gates, they gave way, and Mr. Sweet fled from him, his child, he was the father of the young Heracles, in despair. He longed to see them dead, or stilled in a permanent way, not dead exactly just stilled, the young Heracles and his wife Mrs. Sweet; if only a great hand would just appear and arrest them, the mother and her child, for how she loved the way he could destroy the child-barrier gates, and how she marveled at the way his clever fingers could undo the locks that were childproof, which had been placed on the cupboards and doors and everything else that might pose a life-threatening danger to the young Heracles; how unbelievable to him now and then, to see his beloved Mrs. Sweet—formerly so at any rate, for he must have loved her when they lived all alone and to-gether at 284 Hudson Street without the young Heracles or that daughter, now carefully hidden in his pocket, out of her mother's sight—Persephone was her name—in the thrall of a child, not even that, a baby who could only stagger across the floors from one room to the other, and dismantle the barriers that kept him out of one room from the other, and unlock cabinets that held in them poisonous housecleaning liquids and such, and if he drank them he would be dead. But the young Heracles never drank the poisonous household liquid cleaners, and he never did run into the busy street just at the moment an unthoughtful teenager in a sports car made of graphite, a graduation gift from his parents, two people who were professionals and made a salary that allowed them to make such a gift to that careless boy, their son, was driving by. And his mother, his beloved Mrs. Sweet, loved him more than can be imagined, then or now.

•

Oh, and oh again, during all that time, Now and Then, Mr. Sweet had been making a symphony, composing a piece of music that brought together many different and even conflicting modes of sound: melodies sung by occupants of a cloister, an abbey, in the middle of the Middle Ages, and in these places sex was forbidden but partaken of nonetheless; remnants of riffs (a word, an idea, riffs that Mrs. Sweet did not quite understand) played on the piano by descendants of slaves who, without meaning to, found themselves in New Orleans or a town in Alabama or a town on the banks of the Mississippi River; repeating a coda from Mozart and Bach and Beethoven (or so Mrs. Sweet understood it, but her understanding is not without its misunderstandings), and then the whole thing ended in a calamity of sounds and melodies and emotions and the audience hearing it would rise up from their seats and clap and cheer, for the audience was made up of Mr. and Mrs. Sweet's friends, who were also in the same predicament: only they, each of them, cheered each other on and on in their wild undertakings, trying to portray the known world in a new way and hoping to persuade all its inhabitants, or at least just the people who lived next door (in the Sweets' immediate case, it would be the people who lived in that village in New England), that things—the arts in particular—were in a constant state of flux and this flux was the very essence of living, and living in this way was to be in contact with the ineffable, the divine. And Mr. Sweet had worked away at this symphony, from before the young Heracles was born, during the time Mrs. Sweet carried the young Heracles in her stomach, at great personal cost to her, for she suffered: while in her womb, the young Heracles would often fall asleep contentedly, but in such a way that he pressed against a major nerve ending in her leg, the sciatic nerve; and Mr. Sweet worked away at his symphony of contrasting and contradictory modes of melody and so on, then, now, and also toward the time that then became his now—and it mattered not to him, Mrs. Sweet's discomfort in carrying the young Heracles, and they then and now did not interest the world, his compositions.

•

How Mrs. Sweet loved her husband's creations! When he played them for her on his pianoforte, she did not understand them, this is very true, in the way that Mr.

Sweet understood them when he wrote these master-pieces of music—indecipherable to the mentally back-ward (that would be any person who could not understand the theory of relativity, and Mrs. Sweet was among them), but mind-exploding to their friends—a world made up of Mr. Sweet's friends from even the time be-fore he was born—and Mrs. Sweet so loved Mr. Sweet that she had made herself into an essential part of his Then and wove it into her own: Now. The fugues of boogie-woogie, *dans la sueur*, becoming to her like a ca-lypso, steel band, iron band, the sound of two women quarreling over a man they loved but who did not love them, in the open street in the capital city of an island, the capital city must have a cathedral. How Mr. Sweet became a part of her! And in the way that all the parts of another person whom you love deeply become inter-twined with your own self: their heart with yours, their lips with yours, their fingers and toes with yours, their Now, their then with yours—it is how they and you make children! And then, right then, Mrs. Sweet wept, not from regret but from joy at something she did not understand, and swelled up with feelings of joy and her love for Mr. Sweet, who sat in a little room above a ga-rage all alone, content to make music on the lyre, music that no one wanted to hear, no one in the entire world, not even this wonderful woman, for it was music she could not understand, and had that music been made by her favorite member of the vegetable kingdom she would have considered it a flaw, a flaw being a necessary ingre-dient in perfection and love too. But she so loved Mr. Sweet, the father of her most beloved young Heracles and her most beloved the beautiful Persephone too, a great man, carving something out of nothing, making an entity, an empire of sound—a symphony, a fugue, especially a fugue: polyphonic texture shredded, ribbonlike, a conflagration, and then tones harmonic and expanded and then all wrapped up in a neat procedure! BANG! . . . BANG! . . . BANG! . . . and Mrs. Sweet was down with that, which is the way the young Heracles would put it then, when he would be in his fourteenth year, fifteenth year, and into the years before he went off to college: I'm down with that, by which he meant, "yes," only "yes" and simply "yes!" And that was the word that came into Mrs. Sweet's mind when she thought of Mr. Sweet's fugues and his symphonies and choral presentations and music for four hands playing the piano and music that no one cared about, not even Mr. Sweet, who wrote such music; though he was at once so full of himself, so confident to be exact, and doubt itself or room for doubt never entered his mind. And Mrs. Sweet loved to think how as a child, a Tudor-era-sized child, Mr. Sweet would accompany his mother and father to listen to whole orchestras and choirs playing and singing the music of Johann Sebastian Bach, Amadeus Mozart, César Franck, for she grew up in the time of calypso, with calypsonians who bore names like Lord Executor, Attila the Hun, the Mighty Sparrow, and a steel band with the name Hell's Gate.

•

So Mrs. Sweet loved her husband, their two children—Now, Then—the girl, who Mr. Sweet had made his close companion and kept hidden from Mrs. Sweet among his musical notes; the boy, the young Heracles who was growing so rapidly, outgrowing the need to wear diapers, first of all, then no longer needing to be soothed by the sight of men operating large, noisy machines, no longer excited by the sight of the snowplow as it makes its way through a blizzard, no longer losing his balance if he walked too fast, no longer mispronouncing words, no longer an infant, just a boy, a little boy growing rapidly, his every Now becoming Then, his every Now a Then to be. And she loved them and loved them and thought of her love for them as a form of oxygen, something without which they would die.

But now, regarding Mrs. Sweet and Mr. Sweet then did just that: her voice in particular annoyed him, especially the sound of it, for she liked to sing in the high-pitched way of a boy and she wasn't a boy, she was a woman, and her voice sounded like a boy; she was not a soprano, she was his wife, as common as fish or beef or vegetables on his plate for dinner, or the postman who brought the bills from the household utility companies. Mrs. Sweet could not sing, no one thought her voice, as it suddenly burst into song, a joy, a pleasure, something to long for again; only the young Heracles loved it as she read to him in a singsong way from the books *Goodnight Moon* or *Harold and the Purple Crayon* or *No Jumping on the Bed* and then, he—the young Heracles—would say, "Oh Mom, read that again," and when she did, by the time she came to the end, he was snoring, so loud and in a way that she had never heard before, she would laugh hysterically to herself, but smile, if you were observing her. But most certainly she could not sing in a way that could have pleased Mr. Sweet, a man, who as a boy had been taken to venues by his own mother and father, and they listened to people trained to sing in different modes: alto, soprano, and all the formal rest of that; Mrs. Sweet sang like a milkmaid, like a girl singing to domesticated animals, trying to distract both the animals and the girl from the reality of the situation—life and living and death and dinner! And for Mr. Sweet, her voice and all that it contained, all that it reminded him of, all the things in the world of music as he was educated to know and understand, this singing of hers was a violation: like, synonymous to, as if it were a crime worth bringing before a court of justice composed of the world of culture and civilization, whatever those might be, thought Mrs. Sweet to herself, always to herself, she had such thoughts. The sound of her voice, as she read to the young Heracles, made him want to kill her, take an ax (as a child, he lived in an apartment, and he had never seen such a thing) and chop off her head and then the rest of her body into little pieces, pieces so small that a crow could devour them in pleasure, never having to worry about the size of the morsels he was devouring. Mrs. Sweet's voice, her voice! So nauseating . . . the sound of it often made Mr. Sweet want to empty himself of the contents of his own stomach or remove his stomach altogether but of course he could not live without his stomach; her voice, Mrs. Sweet's voice, so full of love for everything and everybody that she loved, so repulsive to Mr. Sweet, for he did not love her; the sound of her voice reminded him of the sound of a single nail raked along the side of a pane of glass; of the sound of a steel spatula against the bottom of a frying pan, as a perfectly fried egg was removed to a breakfast plate; and with that voice, she liked to sing "Beauty's only skin deep, yeah, yeah, yeah."

•

But now, for Mr. Sweet was still regarding Mrs. Sweet, her voice was like an unwanted alarm clock on a day that fell in the beginning of the week; a red light on the un-interrupted smooth, long, easily manageable curved road through some green mountains—her voice was the red light, irritating and interrupting everything that was pleas-ant: an example being Mr. Sweet's well-being. She was so very annoying, that woman who was his wife, just now, that time after the young Heracles had come into the world: her chest was made up of two sacs filled with milk, and its contents were consumed by that new per-son, the young Heracles; her torso like a very old tree—a silver maple—whose curiously twin trunks were all that remained after a violent storm that cut a broad swathe through a hillside, a dale, a meadow, and such; her broad and fat feet could only fit into her Birkenstock sandals; her head, and that brought to mind her voice, for it re-sided somewhere inside her head—and at the thought of that, Mr. Sweet carefully combed through the many operas, or plays, he knew by heart or his own personal memory—in any case, he hated the sound of her voice as he heard it, talking to him or reading a goodnight story to the children, and he hated the sound of her voice, because she could not sing on key the songs she liked,

"This Old Heart of Mine" in particular, and he hated the sound of her voice for reasons that were not reasonable at all, the sound of delicately cooked tender flesh parts of a cow trapped inside her jaws—she was eating a piece of steak, it was the sound of her chewing. He loved her, oh yes, yes, so he did, and he hated her, especially the way in which she did things, small things, necessary things: like getting out of bed in the middle of the night to pee.

But he used to enjoy her company so, for he had the stature of a prince from the Tudor era and the ability to regard the rest of world as if it existed to satisfy his interests or to be vulnerable to his interests and all his interests belonged to him; yes, yes, in the life of the mind he used to love her and enjoy her way of wearing fruits and vegetables as if they were actual clothes, the way she walked into oncoming traffic, certain that it would halt before it turned her beautiful human form into something mushy, dead, something quickly forgotten; the way she would find the simplest thing extraordinary: she once caught forty-six mice in traps she had set and then could not believe that so many of something she hated and feared could exist; the way she towered over him, not physically, just her presence, her reality, she came from far away, she loved things with spices, she had never eaten grapes, apples, or nectarines when she was a child, she loved and she loved and she loved and Mr. Sweet fell in love with her because of the passion with which she could love all the many things that truly made up her true self, even though nothing about her would make him weigh his very own solid existence and judge himself wanting and decide that his existence, his life, his anything should be secondary to hers. But Mrs. Sweet did not know that, did not know of the ways in which Mr. Sweet's imagination, his Now and his Then, his ways of seeing the present, the past and the future, colored the ways in which he saw her.

Here she is again: her naturally black hair, thick and coarse as ropes that were usually found in the hands of stevedores, cut off so short that she might be mistaken for a stevedore himself, the color of her hair was the color of new rope in the hands of a stevedore—blonde; her eyebrows removed with a razor and in their place a line drawn in the colors: blue—if she felt like it; green, if she felt like it; gold, if she felt like that then; her lips painted red, a red meant to reflect the color of the fires that burnt in one of the many lower circles of hell; her cheeks daubed with an orange goo that was the same color orange as the daylily, *Hemoracallis fulva*, a flower native to China but that now grows wild, unencumbered, without inhibition, in the northeastern part of the United States, an area in which the Sweets lived now, though it was unknown to Mrs. Sweet then, and revolting to Mr. Sweet's consciousness then, and a nightmare for him now! But Then: when Mrs. Sweet was young and so ignorant, she, this lovely person now, then thought that to grow old was a mistake the person who had grown old had made, she thought that all the people who had grown old, had walked through a door, the wrong door, and if only they had chosen the correct door, that thinning and embarrassing folding up of the flesh would not have taken place, they would have continued to be as freshly made as the day they'd turned twenty-one or somewhere around then now, and not be a creaky something, complaining about their failing organs, just the way you do about a car that goes on and on and up and down the roads for a long time and the engine needs a new something, needs many new somethings and the muffler is doomed but can be replaced too and—well, was a person not like that, something useful then, and now not so, but a person was not like a car, a car aged naturally but a person walked through the wrong door: grow old or not! When Mrs. Sweet was young, the not was beyond assuming, like drinking water and not cyanide, and Mrs. Sweet had no true understanding of Now and Now again, and then was in the lower regions of holy grammar. And her youth, before she knew the Tudor-sized prince, Mr. Sweet, was a carnival of sexual activity: all the men on one side, all the women on the other side, dressed in clothes made from the skin of an animal—domesticated or not—or wearing nothing at all, only swirling around to the sound of music coming from a special source or the sound of music which was made up inside their head; and all her youth was a giant atmosphere of sensation, sensation, and sensation again, and her Now (which becomes Then, as is all Now, eventually), she is the mother of the well-hidden beautiful Persephone and the young Heracles and even before that, the wife of Mr. Sweet, a master player of the lyre, is not then known to her; her Now is the scrupulous Mr. Sweet, a man (Tudor prince in size) who understood Wittgenstein and Einstein and all such persons. All such persons!

But Then: in those days when Mrs. Sweet was young and beautiful to him, he then wore shirts and trousers and a navy-blue corduroy jacket, and in the pocket of the navy-blue corduroy jacket was the note from his father, the note that told him how to lead his life: two households, two wives, two sofas, two knives; but he had not found it yet. He then played the pianoforte in a room all by himself, and there was a small audience, then Mr. Sweet, in his full Tudor Princely–ness, would sit down and play some music written by Ferdinand Morton and Omer Simeon and Baby Dodds and Wolfgang Mozart, and if compelled to he would play the music written by his overwhelming favorite, Igor Stravinsky. His mother, a Mrs. Sweet in her own right, was as dutiful and misinformed as Mrs. Sweet—the now Mrs. Sweet, mother to the well-hidden, beautiful Persephone and the young Heracles—adored his performance and led the applause of family and friends, and everyone bowed before him, curtsied, and some of them kissed the ground. Mr. Sweet was then ten years old and for the rest of his life he would be so, ten years old, always in that now moment—that room of playing the music of Ferdinand Morton and sometimes the much-beloved W. A. Mozart, but how was Mrs. Sweet to know that when she fell in love with the young man who bore himself as if he was a young Tudor prince, how was she to know that at thirty years of age, forty years of age, fifty years of age, sixty years of age, seventy years of age, Methuselah's age now, he lived in the world as it was then, when he was ten?

Mrs. Sweet took a deep breath, then and now, and plunged ahead in the dark—for to live in any Now and any Then (they are always the same) is to do just that, plunge ahead in the dark, placing one foot in front of the other—and hoped that there would be some solid, not to mention fruitful, ground to meet her feet, really or metaphorically. As a young woman she had been like a flower found in the deep jungles of the new Americas: a black dahlia, a brown marigold, a sea-green zinnia; when she was a young woman, the world was not her oyster, did not harbor her like its oyster, providing a sweet space in which she became a pearl; when she was a young woman, younger than the young Heracles, it was her fear of death that kept her alive.

•

Plunge ahead or buck up—so Mrs. Sweet's mother would say to her when she was a child, a tall thin girl all bones covered with skin, and she was afraid of the larger girls and the larger than anything boys, and would be so afraid of them that just to walk past them on the street was impossible; and earlier than that, when she was afraid of cows, for no reason at all, only that they were cows and had horns, so she was afraid of them and to walk by a pasture where these animals were fenced in and tethered to iron stakes driven into the ground was impossible for her to do: plunge ahead, put one foot in front of the other, straighten your back and your shoulders and everything else that is likely to slump, buck up and go forward, and in this way, every obstacle, be it physical or only imagined, falls face down in obeisance and in absolute defeat, for to plunge ahead and buck up will always conquer adversity, so Mrs. Sweet's mother had said to her when she was a child, thin in body and soul, and this caused her mother much pain and great shame, for her child—the young Mrs. Sweet—needed to have drummed into her very being the clichéd words of the victorious.

And so: plunge ahead, buck up, aim for a triumphant outcome, death being superior to failure, death is sometimes a triumph, and all this made up the amniotic fluid in which Mrs. Sweet lived when she was a child: in this way Mrs. Sweet learned to drive a car, learned to love the stark realities of her life with Mr. Sweet (he never loved her, not then, not now, she accepted it, now then and now again), took out a loan from the bank to buy the Shirley Jackson house, the house in which they lived, and it was a nice house, with views of mountains and waterfalls and meadows of flowers native to the New England landscape, and farms that cultivated food especially delicious to animals who would then be slaughtered and eaten by someone quite familiar to the slaughtered animals, friends of Mr. and Mrs. Sweet and their children: the young Heracles and the hidden beautiful Persephone; in the far distance, Mrs. Sweet could see the beautiful Mrs. Burley—her long yellow hair in a braid cascading silently down her back and coming to rest just below her shoulder blades—a young cheese-maker milking her cows and her goats, and from this milk she would make some rare cheese and delicious yogurt that Mrs. Sweet would purchase and the rest of her family would hate: Mr. Sweet, because he hated everything about Mrs. Sweet, especially her enthusiasms and these were: growing species of rare flowers from seeds she had gone hunting for in temperate Asia, cooking, and knitting, especially that infernal knitting. Oh Mom! Oh Mom! That would be the sound of the young Heracles. And the love and contempt and indifference that came toward Mrs. Sweet from her beloved young Heracles seemed at once to be as natural as a sweetly cool breeze that will unexpectedly change the mood of a group of people justifiably angry, or a group of people whose every need and expectation is satisfied and still they search for happiness! By that time (then, now, and then again), Mrs. Sweet had buried her past—in the cement that composes memory, even though she knew quite well that cement deteriorates, falls apart, and reveals eventually whatever it was meant to conceal.

Plunge ahead, buck up, and Mrs. Sweet did just that, as she gathered up Mr. Sweet's dropped clothes and the soiled bath towels and the sheets and the children's clothes, blouses from Wet Seal for the beautiful Persephone and trousers from somewhere else she could not pronounce, T-shirts for the young Heracles bought at a store called Manhattan, though it was located in a city far from the actual place known as Manhattan, and all the articles of clothing and dry goods that a seemingly prosperous American family might use. Mrs. Sweet washed all the clothing and other such things in the washing machine (known to her now, but unknown to her then, when she was that easily defeated child) and dried them in a clothes-drying machine and then folded the towels and other such things, and she got out the ironing board and ironed all of Mr. Sweet's shirts and trousers too, for she loved him so, and wanted him to appear to everyone who glimpsed him for the first time as if he had just stepped out of a display in the window of a store called Love: dignified and worthy of respect. All this made her tired, in body and mind equally—the work of it, the imagining of it: clean clothing for two children and Mr. Sweet, making them look as if they lived in a mansion on a prominent street in Manhattan, or as if he lived in a village in New England with a wife and mother who had no idea of how to be her own true self. But to Mrs. Sweet, to whom he was actually and legally wedded, all this was something else: here she is plunging ahead and bucking up too: and walking on air, on nothing visible to the human eye, and she did not fall into oblivion or whatever substance was made to disguise oblivion, and she went on to the next thing and the next thing and the thing after that, and each thing and each nothing she conquered, and she went on in her ways, looking after her husband, tending her children, looking up at the moon (quarter, half, or full) to see if it was in a shroud of clouds (rain tomorrow, in any case), and feeling happy, whatever that is, Then and Now!

5

Mrs. Sweet ended all these thoughts, for the door to the room that was just off the kitchen opened with a mighty force, and Mrs. Sweet knew immediately that it was her son the young Heracles.

The young Heracles would always be so, then, now, and then to come, as would his sister the beautiful Persephone be so, then, now, and then to come. Their mother Mrs. Sweet had deemed it to be that way. But now, just this now, the young Heracles flung open the door to the room just off the kitchen, the room in which Mrs. Sweet kept her true self and had never revealed it to anybody, not Mr. Sweet, not the beautiful Persephone, not the young Heracles, and she had no idea that they knew of her secret communing with her true self and that they viewed this with feelings of various kinds: sympathy from the young Heracles, simple hatred from the beautiful Persephone, homicidal rage from Mr. Sweet. But now, just this now, the young Heracles said to his mother, "Mom, Mom, what are you doing? I've been looking for you all over the place. You weren't in the garden, you weren't in the kitchen, you weren't in bed reading a book no one but you would care about. Where were you? Can Tad, Ted, Tim, Tom, and Tut come over? We wanna play a game but Dad says I better ask you because we're gonna make a lot of noise and he's trying to finish writing his concerto for two pianos for the Troy Orchestra and we're probably gonna make a lot of noise because we don't know how to be quiet, I don't know how to be quiet, I keep telling Dad, I don't know how to be quiet, I don't know how to stay still, I don't know what to do, Mom, Mom are you listening to me, are you listening to me? Help me, Mom, say something, tell me what's going on." Oh how his mother loved him and she thought of the time when he was in her stomach and would not stay still, how all night he jumped up and down in her womb and then would stretch himself to his full height, almost twenty-four inches diagonally, and she could see the imprint of his heel and the imprint of his fist through her skin, as if her skin were a piece of old, worn-out fabric, and then she wanted to say something to him that would make him place himself into that posture of the unborn child in the uterus that decorates the walls of obstetricians' waiting rooms, and that unborn child who fits perfectly in the illustrated pelvic area and develops into a baby without the host knowing of it, and host and child are one but they acknowledge nothing of their unspeakable intimacy, and that intimacy is a lost island that has not yet been found. But so did the young Heracles enter into Mrs. Sweet's very being, distorting the skin of her stomach, bouncing up and down on her sciatic nerve, rupturing

the lining of her cervix so that she had to go to bed for
days and days and she worried that she would never see
his face, his broad nose, his eyes that were the color of
some mineral to be found in distorted rock, his lips like
hers, thick and unparted like night mixed up with day,
his large hands and feet, his hair so thick and curled, the
weight of his head on his shoulders; and then he was
born suffering from jaundice, the blood of his mother
and the blood of his father at war inside him, and that
battle had not ended before he came into this world; for
days he lay in a bassinet under the glare of fluorescent
lights and Mrs. Sweet stayed by his side and fed him food
from her breasts and on the eighth day he was released
and only the blood of his mother remained in his veins.
But Mrs. Sweet thought nothing of this in her everyday
life, only when she was in the little room just off the
kitchen, and the insufferableness of all of them, Mr. Sweet,
the beautiful Persephone, the young Heracles, their de-
mands, their needs, their requests and not one among
them pitied her; why should they? She seemed to sail
along smoothly, magically finding the money to purchase computers powerful enough to employ software
that could arrange and copy complicated musical compositions, or building a lovely little cottage in the woods
where Mr. Sweet could retreat from the disturbance of
those children and the presence of that woman who had
absolutely arrived on a banana boat or some vessel like
that, for nobody knew exactly how she arrived; she had
a story that began with her mother hating her and sending her away to make money to support her family and
she had no father, there was no claim made on her, she

was just sent away on a vessel that went back and forth, carrying cargo, human sometimes, of a nonhuman but commercial nature sometimes, and there she was, this woman who was the mother of his children, a woman from a place far away, a place Mr. Sweet could never visit, for Mr. Sweet would not cross the street if he knew his shadow would accompany him.

But now Mrs. Sweet was very much listening to her sweet son, his voice like an instrument only a boy could play or would want to play, a boy who could summon an army of shy Myrmidons, battalions of archers and sword wielders and spear throwers, all of them borne out of the wrapping of a Happy Meal from McDonald's or Mickey D's or the Sign of the Golden Arches, as the young Heracles would say as it pleased him; there were many Happy Meals and so there were many shy Myrmidons. He said, the young Heracles, in that voice that only his mother could hear, a voice that was so pleasing to her ears, well my dad is a complete asshole, he doesn't know anything, he hates throwing balls and he won't take me to the Basketball Hall of Fame in Springfield, Massachusetts, and I don't even know where that is, and he won't take me to the Baseball Hall of Fame in Cooperstown and I kind of know where that is, and do you know what just happened, he came in and I know he had been with those girls, those really cute student girls who say to him, oh Mr. Sweet, *Pierrot Lunaire* and *Lulu* and I don't know what else but there is something else and he comes in from outside after all this and he says to me: young Heracles, where is my beautiful wife, as if I didn't have a clue about all the time he has been adjusting his corduroy trousers that Mom had bought for him at the Brooks Brothers outlet in Manchester, really cool pants too, but they were too long for him, and when she had them shortened he looked like a short guy wearing somebody else's pants, but that was Dad, my dad, he looked like another guy and I just knew that my dad was someone else and I didn't want him to be anything but someone else, but when he asked me if I had seen his beautiful wife, I said to him, no, but if you are looking for Mom, she is in the garden. And I knew he was going to laugh: Mom wasn't beautiful because she was my mother; Mom wasn't beautiful because she was his wife; and I knew he was going to laugh because it was a funny thing to say, I just knew it and I knew when he laughed he wouldn't notice that I knew he was doing something and I didn't know then what he was doing, I couldn't say, hey Dad, this is what you are doing, you hate me, you hate your wife, you don't think she is beautiful, you hate this house we live in, you hate the garden, you hate the way Mom will just do anything: big things like building a huge stonewall around the house with some stones that she paid someone to haul in a truck from a quarry miles away in Goshen, Massachusetts, and then right after that there was a big quarrel over how to pay for it over dinner and Mom said, but the stones are of mica schist formed 400 million years ago in the Lower Devonian Period and this metaphoric rock, now in shades of rust, gold, blue, black, gray, that will surround the house, making it look afloat, is the result of sandy mud sediments that had been resting at the bottom of an ancient sea, and Dad didn't say anything else, he just continued to eat his food, and Mom had cooked poached veal with tuna fish sauce and Italian rice with shredded basil and mozzarella cheese and a salad, and Dad just hated Mom, she was becoming fat then, she had taught me to make her a martini and she would sit in the garden at the end of the day, in the middle of all those flowers that Wayne and Joe gave her, some flowers that they said looked great in their garden but they looked terrible in Mom's garden, they grew all over the place like weeds, as if they hadn't been given instructions in how to grow in another place other than in Reads-boro, Vermont, and Dad was happy to see her disap-pointments and me too, especially me too, for I wanted her to be Mom and didn't want to have to go to Clear-brook Farm to buy her a six-pack of celosia for Mother's Day, just after Dad dumped her because he had fallen hopelessly in love with a woman younger than Mom, a woman that he felt made him understand his true, true self.

Is Mom an error, and if she is what should I do with her, rub her out like when I'm in school and I make my letters not so good? Is Mom a mistake and can I cor-rect her? Is Mom a disaster, like when the wind blows too hard, or when the rain comes too much, or when the rain doesn't come at all for years and years? Is Mom a disaster? Jesus Christ, and that was the voice of Mrs. Sweet, shredding the air itself, if such a thing could be done, and she sprinted across the lawn that had just been mowed by Mr. Pembroke or someone who worked for him, and she stretched out her already unusually long arms, as if she were one of the transformers, the toys that were not yet part of the everyday life of the young Heracles, and she removed him from the path of the speeding vehicle, a red Nissan sports car being driven by a boy, a junior at the Mount Anthony Union High School, a member of a sports team where speed of foot is highly valued, a boy whose mother worked in a factory not far away in which fabric made from barrels of petroleum was sewed into something that might be worn or sat upon or contain food in such a way that a person on eating it will think of the word fresh, but only the word fresh will actually be fresh, and it was in this moment that the young Heracles was removed from death's door, and his mother, the delightful and much-despised Mrs. Sweet, who could from time to time be despicable and just plain awful, hugged him to her close and wished the boy driver a fiery death, and later when he did die and not at all because of anything having to do with that swift red sports car made of fiberglass but because of an unexpected rupture of an artery somewhere in his head, the dear Mrs. Sweet wept for his mother, not for him but for the boy's own mother.

And those tears she wept then were so much, so much, so much, and they might be the beginning of a sea that might be ancient eventually, but just then, right now, they were absorbed into the bib of her overalls that had been purchased from the Gap or through the Smith & Hawken catalog, depending, and the tears that began the sea that would eventually become ancient remained just tears, and Mrs. Sweet gathered the young Heracles to her bosom and was so glad that just then she had avoided the face of sorrow and the immediacy of sorrow and also had avoided becoming intimate with that dreadful entity, that world: sorrow; and those tears she wept then and now, Now being constant and unchangeable and liable to make foolish all that insists on being held permanently dear, Then being like the earth's surface with its crust seemingly fixed and stable to all who need it to be so, those tears were absorbed in her mom garment and also were in the great world of water and all that might be vulnerable to it.

All the same, there was the young Heracles, saved from being made dead by the boy who did not listen to his mother when she warned him about all the dangers of the world, who would have died at nineteen years of age anyway, even if he had listened to his mother, from some unexpected malfunction in his body; and that mother had loved that boy and would have reached into her son's body to mend it and make his life a long life, a life that continued after hers ended, for she could see herself absent in his world but couldn't imagine him absent from hers, now or then. Mrs. Sweet saw all that, standing over a bed of lettuce that would soon bolt and Shep, who sometimes helped her to move full-grown trees from one place to another, was now speaking to her, and as she watched his lips move, she heard herself only: Where are the Oberleys? For Shep has, this year, a spectacular crop of beans that we all must taste; Gordon has made Ann a dry riverbed; Mrs. Sweet's friends Dan and Robert who live in Heronswood, Washington, has sent her a batch of their white double-flowering helle-bores; and then, only then, she heard the words that made Shep's lips move: By the way, did you mean to park the car in the grove of white pines that has been purposely sited at the entrance of the pond, and just then the threshold of her life disappeared for she saw the middle-aged Kuniklos, a car made in Germany, a country that had transgressed the human bond to such a degree that it could not be discussed in the intimacy of a kitchen or even the indifferent atmosphere of a restaurant, and the car had come to a rest in the grove of white pines, a grove of trees that had not been removed because their presence in the landscape of an expansive field was pleasing to the eye of the owner of the field, and the owners were Gordon and Ann. The young Heracles was all strapped up in his car seat, and the car seat itself firmly fixed to the middle seat in the back of the car, all these precautions recommended by authorities devoted to the prevention of sorrow and despair of a particular kind; but he had removed himself from the car seat and climbed over to the driver's position, seated himself, and turned the key to the ignition, but he had never seen the maneuvering of the driver's feet, and so the car jumped forward and jumped forward and jumped forward and came to a halt in the grove of pines, instead of breaking the surface of that beautiful pond and eventually sinking to its stinking bottom, for the bottom always stinks. And when the grower of the beans, Shep, said those words, by the way did you guys mean to park the car down near the pond, Mr. and Mrs. Sweet, the father and mother of the young Heracles, knew everything that had happened, every motion, and thought of him, knew it as it happened, knew it before it happened, but did not know the end, and they leapt out of themselves and ran toward him, not knowing if they would find him dead or alive, but they did find him and he was alive in the car, trying without success to open the doors and get out into other adventures, which might be cleaning the fabled Augean Stables, slaying the Nemean Lion and wearing its skin as a cloak, an encounter with the Erymanthian Boar, though not yet and perhaps never the policeman in the city of Boston, who traces himself through some long-dead people from Ireland, imagines that the young Heracles has run through a red light and by that time, then and now, the young Heracles had become a young black man, whatever that might be, and even now, whatever that might be is not certain.

•

Oh now, oh then, but see him now, that would be the young Heracles, with the chicken pox he caught from his sister the beautiful Persephone and their mother Mrs. Sweet caught it from them both and it made her unable to breathe properly, for her lungs were covered with little blisters even as she appeared without blemish; and see him now with the other children in their striped overalls and white turtleneck, with the words OshKosh embroidered on these garments, so discreetly that it wasn't discreet at all, swinging a toy hammer, or a toy version of every tool useful to a carpenter or a plumber or a farmer, a toy version of such an individual, for neither did Mr. and Mrs. Sweet nor any of the other parents imagine that these children would become in real life a carpenter, a plumber, a farmer, but what these children would become was not a question that was ever asked then and so

cannot be answered now; and the children, that would
be the young Heracles and the beautiful Persephone, did
really love their mother then and would miss her terribly
when she left the house to do something they found incomprehensible, read out loud those words she had committed to paper while dwelling in that awful room off
the kitchen, the room to which they had no access, not
even if they took a boat or a plane or a car or a hike, not
at all could they reach her when she was in that room off
the kitchen, and then how they loved her, but she was
apart from them and only in the world of those sentences: "I have the most sensible suitcase in New York, I
have the most sensible small car in New York" and "My
mother died at the moment I was born, and so for my
whole life there was nothing standing between myself
and eternity; at my back was always a bleak, black wind"
and "There is a chamber in the life of the gardener that
is not a place in the garden at all." Oh Mom, oh Mom,
where are you, cried the young Heracles and the beautiful Persephone, not at all in unison, for their mother was
lost to them but never at the same time, and the young
Heracles in particular missed her, and had always missed
her for even when he was a baby and she nursed him he
wasn't with him at all and he would look up into her
face and then into her eyes and she looked down on him
but it was as if he were a picture of a little baby nursing
at his mother's breast and he would sink his little baby
teeth into her breast and then it yielded only her flesh,
the milk was diminishing, she wanted it so, and the flesh
of her breast was like the wheel of a tire but he had no

idea of a tire then, and when he bit her, her annoyance at his presence grew, at his very appearance in her life, she had forgotten that he was her beloved and only son, for then he was simply an animal biting her in the breast, like a serpent or some other small invertebrate that would be a symbol of the great decline of humankind, and how she wished he wouldn't hurt her so, and how he wished that his mother would look at him as she nursed him; Oh Mom, oh Mom, where are you? asked the children of the dear Mrs. Sweet and they asked this of her as if she could not ever have been in need of such a thing herself, a mom! A mother!

But the young Heracles recovered from all the childhood diseases that might have killed his mother when she was a child in that friendly banana-growing entity in which she grew up but which she, without any known explanation, survived, and this fact, her survival, could and was often used as an epithet hurled at her, she survived tropical illness and now lived in a climate in which such vulnerability was known only in proper literature which she would like to write, poor woman, said her husband to himself! And all that should be put aside, for it is then, even as it is now, and the young Heracles was wading through the time when he was prescribed a medicine that made bumps the size of an infant's fist appear on his body, and the doctor said to Mrs. Sweet that such a thing only occurred in one person out of a million, and Mrs. Sweet was so made speechless by this that she took the young Heracles to Key West, Florida, and there he met a man who wrote five books and in each book one of the vowels was absent.

But the young Heracles grew and grew in strength, wisdom not immediately because sometimes he was said to be suffering from a deficit in his ability to concentrate and sometimes he was said to be unable to comprehend the variety of ways the known world was presented to him and sometimes he was said to be suffering from a variety of rapidly changing bad moods, but he only caused suffering to the shy Myrmidons, who were lined up and poised to join him in battle against the Ninja Turtles, and the young Heracles took turns leading these hordes of warriors against each other and which was the winning side always depended on the side he favored then, right then, right now. And his arms and feet became retractable then but his dear mother only discovered this when one day, while she was sowing a field with *Asclepias* with seed purchased from a mysterious seed-man named Hudson whose address was somewhere in Los Angeles, and she wondered how to heal her sweet son, she saw his arms stretch out from his body, up, up into the clear air, below the blue sky and through some white clouds and his fingers came to rest on the bare spot, a smooth cliff, that was a feature of the mountain called Bald, and he would remove small parts of the cliff and place them at his feet and then hit them across the lawn, as if they were golf balls bought in bulk from the store nearby. That bare spot on the mountain was miles and miles away, and as he extended his arm he made a sweet low whistling sound and different species of sparrows settled on it, Mrs. Sweet heard him call out softly: *Spizella pusilla, Pooecetes gramineus, Passerculus sandwichensis, Ammodramus savannarum, Melospiza lincolnii* and then he sang a series of tunes that were exactly like the birds' tunes themselves, and Mrs. Sweet marveled at this, for it is well known that her poor little boy could not carry a tune and had been asked by his piano teacher not to attend class anymore, for along with being a disruptive presence, he had no ear at all, that is, no ability to imitate and reproduce B flat; and his mother, that would be the dear Mrs. Sweet, said to him, how can you do that, how do you know their songs? and her son said, I know it because I taught it to them, they only know how to do that because I showed them Mom, I showed them. And what else can you do, she said, not asked, what else can you do, she said, and the young Heracles said, I can kill a lion and make a coat to wear when I go skiing out of his skin, and I can kill the Lernaean many-headed monster that could kill you if you saw it in a dream, and I can kill a wild boar, and I can kill the Stymphalian Birds, all of them, because I am not afraid of them, and I can clean the Augean Stables, and I can capture the Cretan Bull, I can't stop Dad from wanting to kill me, that's just the way he is. I can't stop myself from killing him, I'm going to kill him and he will never know because I can't let him know, he would be so disappointed, he is already so disappointed, his disappointment would be complete and I really love him so I don't want him to see that, but I am going to kill him, he has to die, we all have to die, right Mom, right Mom? Oh Mom, oh Mom, said the young Heracles, are you going to cry and remind me of how Dad stayed up with me and watched Michael Jordan play in the championships when Jordan had the flu, and when he made a basket he would fall down but Scottie Pippen would run up and rescue him from falling to the ground, are you going to do that, Mom, are you going to say, oh, it was so Homeric, the way Scottie and Dennis played, and Malone was such a Hector and Stockton was so Paris: oh the whole thing was so Homeric, and you would say this over and over until I wanted to throw you overboard but we were not in a sea or anything, we were just in the house in which Shirley Jackson used to live.

Oh Mom, oh Mom, so said the young Heracles, he spoke to her in that way, calling her name twice, for to him Mrs. Sweet's name was Mom: oh Mom, oh Mom: and Mrs. Sweet shrank into a ball, the size of a ball of some kind or another that is to be met on the side of the road by accident, and she shrank into the size of a ball that is seen in a basket, one of many, in a store that is filled with things that are not related to balls at all: oh Mom, oh Mom, tell me all the things that happened before you were even born, and he laughed, his laugh was golden, as if it defined that man-made value itself, as if the value of gold had been determined by the laugh of the young Heracles, and Mrs. Sweet sat down, or did something like that, came to a complete halt that was apart from standing, and she looked at her son and adored him, he was so precious and wise, for by then he had absolutely refused to swallow the small white tablets of Adderall; oh Mom, oh Mom, tell me the marriage story tonight when I go to sleep in the bed that Cadmus and Harmony gave you, the bed that was from the time before Cadmus changed his name and that was so cool when we used to go trick-or-treating and Cadmus was all disguised as a woman but now, right now, he really is a woman but then he was just Cadmus and that was so cool and he would come by the Shirley Jackson house and drink rum with you; oh Mom, oh Mom, tell me the marriage story.

And Mrs. Sweet said to him, no, no, and she was horrified and had never told him the story of Mr. Sweet and how they met on the seventeenth floor of an apartment building when she was twenty-seven years old on the week before Christmas, and she had always hated Christmas when she was a child, because she grew up in a place not too far from the equator and Christmas is a holiday that is best understood and appreciated if you live much farther north of the equator, and how surprised she was that this idea, Christmas, so special in her imagination when she was a child, was then and now so full of anxiety: partings and closings and partings again, and gifts of things and kisses and then silences, great silences, and food eaten but no loudness, nothing, as if Christmas were a death, a mourning, a funeral, and then they all went to bed. And then thirty days after that we met again and we didn't even remember that, for we slept in the same bed and we went to see Twyla Tharp and we went to a rehearsal of an orchestra that was perfecting the *Goldberg Variations* and would later that evening perform in front of an audience; it was then I understood the Long Rain, a period of my life when I was a child and all events seemed to have no end and no beginning at all but certainly no end, for they were only now, and it is only just right now in speaking of them that they become Then, as if the past only becomes past when you render it Now; and the rush on my part to belong to someone who knew the world in ways that were unknown to me, being and not being, was how I came to marry your father. Oh sweet darling, dearest young Heracles, but I couldn't call out to you then and I can only call out to you now because I needed you then but not so now, never now, always only then, said the dear Mrs. Sweet, reading to the young Heracles a chapter from a book called *See Then Now*, against her better judgment, that is, without her really meaning to do so. And she went on, for she was unable to stop, the pages of that book compelled her to continue, her eyes were glued to them, her tongue was an ingredient of the pages, her own mind made the physical presence of the book possible even as she held it in her own hands: in those days your father, Mr. Sweet, was a very good person, not this grizzled, graying, impotent man you see now who stalks the woods afraid of everything, liking only the trees that have been made dead in a storm; in those days, he was only afraid of the streets of lower Manhattan early in the morning or late at night, for in those days those streets were without people, all the people lived somewhere else, they only worked in those streets and then they went home; but we lived in the places where people only worked and your father hated me for making him live in these places but he didn't know he hated me yet, he didn't know that his feelings for me were not feelings of love, they were feelings of hatred; and I loved him, for he was so full of knowledge of Beethoven and Bach and Shostakovich and Stravinsky and Schoenberg and Alban Berg . . . but we were not married yet, we were not Mr. and Mrs. Sweet then, we would only become that when you, the young Heracles, and the beautiful Persephone, were born, before that we were not anything, we were only possibilities of Mr. and Mrs. Sweet, without the birth of the young Heracles and the birth of the beautiful Persephone we would not be and so become: Mr. and Mrs. Sweet. Oh Now, oh Then, but even before then, we had become Mr. and Mrs. Sweet because I was living in the United States of America without proper papers and could have been sent back to that small island from which I came, an island that is so small, history now only records it as a footnote to larger events and the larger events are even now footnotes, and before your father married me and I was vulnerable to deportation, George said to Sandy, you know one of us will have to marry Jamaica, and all went on in that way until your father married me and Veronica did not attend the ceremony and Sheila threw rice at us, which she had bought at a market on upper Broadway, and your aunt forgot to turn off the stove with the coffee on the burner and she had to go back home from the ceremony and turn the stove off because the place in which they lived could have caught fire and your grandfather couldn't go in an elevator and the judge was so kind and he came down from his chamber and officiated at the marriage and your father and mother were then married and your mother didn't have to be forcibly repatriated to the backwater banana entity from which she came, so Mr. Sweet was thinking but kept to himself, and your father and mother, to whom you, the young Heracles and the beautiful Persephone, were unknown as if you were nothing and nothing again, not even worthy of a capital letter, nothing, take a breath, a pause here, said Mrs. Sweet, and she held the book in her hand and wanted to rest it on her knees, but did not.

Oh Mom, oh Mom, did not say the young Heracles, for his eyes were closed, for he was not asleep, for he was not awake, for he was only listening to his mother read a book to him just before he fell asleep, and this was a time long after *Goodnight Moon* and *The Runaway Bunny* and *No Jumping on the Bed* and *Harold and the Purple Crayon*, long, long after all that and all those books were only lodged in Mrs. Sweet's memory because in those days the children were her captives and could only be consoled by her droning on in her inimitable droning, as if she were an announcer on the BBC airwaves as heard in the British West Indies.

6

It was in the middle of that night, way, way into the middle of that night, fifteen minutes into the new day, that the beautiful Persephone was born. And her birth, her arrival in that world of the room in the hospital, with big bright lights and lots of shouting from people who were commanding Mrs. Sweet to push and push out the baby from her womb, that moment, that now of the beautiful Persephone's arrival into the world, made all of the months before she became the baby who cried as she emerged from her mother's insides, disappear, that time when Dr. Fuchs examined Mrs. Sweet's uterus and found a fibroid, round in shape like a fruit, with a stout stem anchoring it to that pear-shaped soft organ, and the fibroid after he removed it weighed fifteen and three quarter ounces and this was before the time Mrs. Sweet became a gardener herself and so could not see then, as now, could not see anything at all, not that the thing growing on her uterus was prophetic or a metaphor. But

that time just then, just now, before the beautiful Persephone was born, and before that, before she was even
conceived, Dr. Fuchs removed the growth that was the
size of a well-grown tomato like "Prudence Purple" and
Dr. Fuchs wore clogs and moved about in the maternity
ward at New York Hospital, as if he were meant to do
that, and he told Mrs. Sweet, who was not yet that, for she
would only become that when she possessed her children,
that she would become pregnant, and soon, three months
after, Mrs. Sweet felt ill and thought she was suffering
from an unusual attack of anxiety and so took so many
doses of medicines meant to reduce the feeling of wanting to throw up and the feeling of wanting to make still
the flutterings which were not her heart in her upper
chest and then one day, in April it was, in the middle of
a late snow falling in Londonderry, Vermont, the woman
who was married to a man, a doctor himself, who was a
figure of fun to Mrs. Sweet, for he had a silly mustache
and wore tweeds and it all made him look as if he was a
character in a Penguin paperback published in England
in the 1950s, and it was his wife who told Mrs. Sweet
that she wasn't anxious or suffering from a seasonal dis-
ease, she said that Mrs. Sweet was pregnant, and Mrs.
Sweet then drove through the unplowed roads, swerv-
ing and skidding, avoiding the pond at the sharp turn of
the road that led to the bridge and went into the rented
apartment above the garage of Jill's house and called Mr.
Sweet and said, I am pregnant, and Mrs. Sweet, then,
did not resist this unexpected turn in her life, but it
frightened her, for she vomited constantly, and then

when that stopped she still felt as if she wanted to vomit constantly and that feeling never went away at all, not until that time when the beautiful Persephone was born; and Mrs. Sweet craved grapefruits and then immediately threw up after she ate them but all the same couldn't avoid the craving, which if it was not satisfied would not lead to her throwing up, but a craving in such a circumstance is unavoidable; and she saw a film about some creatures called gremlins and threw up after that, lots and lots of vomit all over the floor of the little apartment where she lived, an apartment built for a boy who was so well situated in life and who was so ill suited to be well situated in life that he joined the army, and while a passenger in a military jeep he had a catastrophe and it left him crippled from the neck down, and this boy's mother built him a house to accommodate his new feebleness; and it was in their house that Mrs. Sweet bore and carried the beautiful Persephone, who was perfect.

●

Then, though it was Now, Then was Now: Mrs. Sweet was lying on a stretcher in a room and Dr. Fuchs, a man who may have invented the amniocentesis test or not, held in his hand a wandlike instrument and he moved it back and forth across her stomach with a childlike glee (so Mrs. Sweet thought then and now), and a childlike intensity, as if defying all his years of learning and acquiring knowledge, as if masking a deep need to, from time to time, repeat actions that were without any obvious meaning but mysteriously significant all the same; and as he did this, move the wandlike instrument back and forth across her stomach, he could see, on a monitor, the beautiful Persephone (not yet beautiful, not yet Persephone), a shaped mass of filaments and membranes and jelly-like stuff, moving relentlessly, moving without pause, in a large amount of water, which Dr. Fuchs knew to be amniotic fluid; he could see the beautiful Persephone's hands, already large, the fingers long and then tapering off into the not known, her legs short, her head a normal size and hairless, her torso a normal size. And then he plunged a large needle into Mrs. Sweet's slightly swollen belly and withdrew some of the amniotic liquid and he was pleased that this whole procedure posed no danger at all to the beautiful Persephone. Then also, Mr. Sweet, who had accompanied Mrs. Sweet into that room in which Mrs. Sweet lay on a stretcher, could make out the image of the beautiful Persephone on the monitor, not immediately, only after a while, only after his eyes got used to the dark and the color of the fluid in which the beautiful Persephone (though then not beautiful and not yet Persephone) existed. And immediately, on seeing her, Mr. Sweet loved his daughter and so therefore she was beautiful and she was new, and her newness was not yet original, not unique, the beautiful Persephone was like a season, spring—just for instance—and spring especially! The dear Mr. Sweet, on seeing the remnants (for we are all made of remnants) that was then all there was of the beautiful Persephone, floating about serenely in the amniotic fluid contained in a sac, which lay within Mrs.

117

Sweet's womb, immediately conceived a symphony of sounds, inspired by her appearance, an evocation and tribute to the simple fact of renewal, whether it be the seasons, spring in particular, whether it be the life cycle of an amphibian, whether it be the skin covering his own being: there was a cycle of living fully and then a decline into death for a while and then living fully in joyousness again. The beautiful Persephone, in utero, catapulted Mr. Sweet into the cycle of living joyously and as if living joyously would and could last forever. He could see immediately, so Mr. Sweet said and thought also to himself, that her fingers, long and strong, were perfectly fit to play the lyre and already—Then, Now—he could hear her renditions of variations of this and that; her renditions, by way of the lyre, of concertos, quartets, quintets, suites, and all other such things. And then Mr. Sweet worried that the beautiful thing swimming around in Mrs. Sweet's womb would be born too soon, before it had spent the usual nine months in utero, and then its brain might not be fully developed and those fingers might fall short of the lengths required of fingers to play the lyre properly and its digestive track might not work properly, and Mrs. Sweet was sent to bed and sang—to herself and to the beautiful Persephone also, who was not yet beautiful or even Persephone, yet— songs she knew from her own childhood: "Two pence ha'penny woman, lie dun on the Bristol, de Bristol e' go go bum-bum, an e' knock out she big fat pum-pum!" And the beautiful Persephone—for after a while she was really becoming beautiful and Persephone, at that—grew and grew to perfection in her mother's womb and then one day, in autumn, she was born.

Say Now about then:

•

At the time that the beautiful Persephone was born, three years and nine months before the birth of the young Heracles, Mr. and Mrs. Sweet lived in the greengrocer's house, just above the Holland Tunnel, and that house, built in the middle of the nineteenth century, by the time the Sweets lived in it had been stripped of any niceness: it had no plumbing and no proper walls, it was hollowed out and they had to make repairs to it, and get permission to run water lines and gas lines and electric lines and exterminate because at least forty-five mice lived in that house. Then Mrs. Sweet grew large, so large that Mr. Sweet, as a joke, meaning to keep her spirits up, for she was in despair at her ballooning figure, as she saw herself in a mirror, began to call her Charles Laughton, and by that he was referring to the actor who had once been married to the actress Elsa Lanchester, but then he (Mr. Sweet) was not thinking of actor or actress, he was not thinking of the person and the impersonation, he was, in his real heart and mind, thinking: my wife is pregnant, there is a person to come inside her and this person is someone I do not want to know, do not want to become part of me, I am not capable of such intimacy, a baby, a child, a person, how to make all of this go away, how to remain myself (by that he meant Mr. Sweet) if this being must come into existence; and Mr. Sweet thought: How happy I am to be the father of this beautiful girl, who will play duets with me, for I will write for her music to be played on the pianoforte, music for four hands, and I will call them Nocturnes for the Beautiful Persephone, I will call all of them Nocturnes for the Beautiful Persephone. I shall love her very much and will keep her close to my heart. Mr. Sweet smiled at his wife, who was in a constant state of throwing up, and she threw up all the contents of her stomach, over and over again and sometimes she felt as if she had thrown up her stomach itself.

But she did not throw up her stomach itself and eventually the beautiful Persephone grew in it and one day she was born. The beautiful Persephone was beautiful, without doubt: her face itself, each part, each aspect of it, was in perfect proportion to the other: the eyes themselves were exactly alike in shape and size and set apart on either side of the bridge of her petal-like nose; her mouth, like the beginning of the moon, before it reached fully, the first quarter; her ears like the shell that had protected some delicate morsel that lived in the bowels of the sea and then died on the shore; she was beautiful, thought her mother and her father, and they then had no inkling that all mothers and fathers everywhere, on seeing their firstborn child, said to themselves: love is beautiful, beauty is perfect and just. As the beautiful Persephone emerged from Mrs. Sweet's womb, she was, then and now, beautiful, and on seeing her covered in vernix caseosa, Mrs. Sweet fell into a violent trembling, she wanted to run away, far away, but she could not, for Dr. Fuchs placed the beautiful Persephone in her arms and he was so pleased because he imagined that he had made three people very happy: the mother and father and the newborn child. In her fit of trembling, her body shaking as if it would shortly exit to the next world, Mrs. Sweet held on to the newly born girl as if she were a lifeline to her own existence, and indeed so it was. And Mrs. Sweet was so afraid that because she was in such a state she would drop her baby on the floor of the delivery room of the hospital in which the beautiful Persephone had just been born, and on falling to the floor, the baby Persephone would shatter and scatter all over, pieces of her lying here and there; and just before she entered a state of panic, of unreasonableness, Mr. Sweet removed the baby from her arms and swaddled her in a blanket provided by the hospital and took her to the nursery and placed her in a bassinet, where she fell asleep among many other babies that had been born just around the same time. Of course, the beautiful Persephone had opened her lungs by crying upon emerging entirely from Mrs. Sweet's body (she had been living parasitically off Mrs. Sweet as she lay growing contentedly in that dear woman's womb) and then she fell deeply asleep and in that sleep she became the beautiful Persephone, again and again and forever. The beautiful Persephone, for she was that by then, needed nutrients, so true, so true, for she could not exist all by herself taking in only the air for breathing, and Mrs. Sweet took her and placed the full sacks of milk that lay indifferently on her chest into the mouth of the beautiful Persephone, who drank and drank, making noises as she did so: amounting to quartets, suites, a monody, a solo, a duo, orchestral, symphonic, a combo of every sound imaginable in harmony, pleasing and pleasurable to a listener of such things, but frightening to someone sitting next to her mother, and that was Mr. Sweet.

The postnatal Mrs. Sweet, that is the mind and body that was then Mrs. Sweet, existed in the faintest circle of a hell not recognized in any of the scriptures. Her body, from her head to her toes, had blown up in a pleasing way to someone: Mr. Sweet continued to lovingly call her Charles Laughton, but when she saw a reflection of herself in the mirror (while brushing her teeth in the bathroom, for instance), her hair unwashed and needing a touch-up, she looked like his wife, the actress Elsa Lanchester, in particular when she portrayed the young bride of the hero Frankenstein. All the same, "Yum, yum, yum" were the sounds then echoing from the mouth of the beautiful Persephone as she tugged at the nipples of Mrs. Sweet's breasts, devouring loudly the milk coming out of them in a rush, and the flow of the milk would have drowned her if Mrs. Sweet had not been paying close attention. Looking up at her mother's face, which was also perfectly round and bulbous, the beautiful Persephone fell in love with the entire being of her mother, without knowing love is accompanied by hatred and contempt, too—which is a benign form of hatred. In any case, how the beautiful Persephone loved her mother, the sweet Mrs. Sweet, the sweetest of all the Mrs. Sweets there had been and the sweetest of all the Mrs. Sweets that might come: her round and full breasts, her round and full face, a glistening brown altogether; her eyes the color of barrels full of molasses, her nose swelling out like a chipmunk's, his cheeks full of chestnuts, or a mongoose's, his cheeks filled with any amphibians or weaker mammals he finds in his way; her lips wide and fat, like the spout of an already large-petaled flower (the hibiscus); her ears large and soft and unusual and remarkable but bearing no likeness to anything in the animal or vegetable kingdom. And so the beautiful Persephone came to fall in love with her mother, the sweet and kind Mrs. Sweet, as she drank from the sacs of milk that lay on her mother's chest. And the beautiful Persephone grew beautiful and beautiful and even so, more beautiful again.

•

Immediately after the beautiful Persephone's birth, Mr. Sweet began to secrete her; first he took her for a walk around the block, placing her in a pouch designed and manufactured by a woman who lived somewhere in California; then he took her for a walk to a park, an emptied-out space near the elevated West Side Highway, and then he took a walk to somewhere, and eventually he took her on a walk, just that, a walk, so that soon a walk became a destination all by itself. Where is she? Mrs. Sweet would ask herself and Mr. Sweet too, if she managed to see him; from her own self came no answer, for she really did not know what happened to the beautiful Persephone, and when she turned to Mr. Sweet he would only smile and say to her, "Hmmmmmh!" and that "Hmmmmmh!" humming to himself, the first few bars of a symphony, a suite, a quartet, a quintet, or so on, predictable as the natural order of things as they would appear in the sphere in November and December, the stars that could be seen in all their glory, if you were standing on the lawn of the Shirley Jackson house and if you were looking up, overhead could be seen the galaxy Andromeda and inside it a bright light called the Great Nebula and nearer still the Magellanic Clouds and Fornax and Draco and Ursa Minor, among other things to be seen overhead; and also Perseus and Cassiopeia and Mirfak and Algol; all this could be observed if you were standing on the lawn just outside and beyond the Shirley Jackson house, but when the beautiful Persephone was born the Sweets then lived in the old house that was built just above the Holland Tunnel, right next to Canal Street.

The beautiful Persephone grew strong and big, so big that she looked like an illustrated rabbit, caught, just before he was cooked, which would then satisfy the hunger of a small family named McGregor; she walked, one step forward before falling, two steps forward, and balancing herself and staying upright, and then all across the kitchen floor while at the same time talking not to herself and not to anyone in particular—Mr. and Mrs. Sweet were the only witnesses—only shouting out, "I might see the moon, I might see the moon," but it was in the middle of the day and they, all three of them, were standing in the kitchen and the windows in the kitchen were few. And Mrs. Sweet hardly saw her apart from the times when she was feeding from the fat sacs filled with milk that grew on Mrs. Sweet's chest, and then that time when she ate a stew of finely ground-up meat and zucchinis for the first time and Mr. Sweet was angry that Mrs. Sweet had not grown the cow and vegetables from scratch, she had only bought this concoction in a jar from the store and on the jar was printed the word "Beechnut." The beautiful Persephone grew and grew and grew, so much did she do so that then she grew out of her mother's reach, for Mrs. Sweet often could not find her, even when she was sitting in front of her at a distance between a beautiful flower and the hand that will pluck it from the stem on which it is naturally growing; Mrs. Sweet could not find her daughter, that beautiful girl who was born at a quarter past midnight, just after Mrs. Sweet had been given an epidural, that beautiful girl with eyes the shape of flying fish seen near the coast of Barbados. So then, in grief, Mrs. Sweet imposed on herself a great silence, and she made a world of it, this silence, and this world was made up of silence: no words could be heard if spoken; no food could have taste if eaten; the skunk, which is not in the rodent family, could not be seen on the endlessly expanding road in twilight as it was run over by a motorcar, and its foul stink, which was often essential in perfumes designed to mask the foul stink of the human body, fell into this silence. A great silence: a silence so great that it was beyond capitalization! In her grief, she grew fat and debauched-looking, like that actor Charles Laughton and also his wife, the actress Elsa Lanchester, she grew to look like them as they appeared in real life or their impersonations, it did not matter, to her or to anyone observing the situation. Then, a great silence overcame Mrs. Sweet and she wept and wept and then wept some more and after that, she turned her world black with ice, for Mr. Sweet had taken her daughter and placed her in the pocket of his jacket, the one that his wife had purchased from the Brooks Brothers outlet store in Manchester, not the one that was identical to the one his own father wore and that was purchased from J. Press on Madison Avenue, and he kept her there for a long time and for all that time Mrs. Sweet never saw the sun shining.

7

That afternoon, at exactly quarter to four, the beautiful Persephone and the young Heracles got off the school bus and found that their mother, the dear Mrs. Sweet, was not waiting to pick them up. They saw the school bus, driven by the madly named Mr. Strange, disappear around the corner below the Bennington Monument; they saw their companions, some wayward boys and girls who lived in villages that were surrounded by evergreens of every kind except for broadleaf, and the evergreens were all sick with a blight of rust; and these companions were very bad, for sometimes the boys among them pummeled the young Heracles almost to death, and the discipline he required to restrain himself from gathering them up altogether in his large brown hands and making them as lifeless as his old socks was greater than the force he had used to smite the entire city of Thebes as it appeared in his handheld Nintendo game; those boys in any case had names of no distinguished origin, their names being Tad, Ted, Tim, and such. But the bus stop was empty of

Mrs. Sweet and the young Heracles was beside himself with anxiety and sorrow, for he loved his mother so and only so; and a dark cloud full of a toxic fire emerged from his forehead and he directed it toward the top of the Bennington Monument, a structure that was dedicated to a battle that led to a defeat and a triumph and the defeated and the triumphant were now settled into the normal disfigurement of everyday living, and he caused it to fall to the ground, just missing a bus full of citizens from Germany, who were taking a tour of New England just then.

So beside himself was the young Heracles with anger and grief over Mrs. Sweet not being there to greet him when the school bus arrived at the bus stop that he sank to the ground, drew his feet up into his chest, his chin resting on his knees, so that he looked like an illustration of a fully developed child intact in his mother's womb, an illustration commonly found on the walls of a doctor's office. Oh come on! And that was the voice of the beautiful Persephone, his sister, and that is as it should be, for it was spring and she was released from living in the depths of the pocket of Mr. Sweet's old Brooks Brothers tweed jacket (and the lining of that pocket was made of silk purchased in Hong Kong). Not knowing what else to do, she lifted him up with much ease, as if he were some just-harvested asparagus, or a pint of strawberries, or a plate of peas, or as if she were removing the hamster that had died overnight in its cage, and she placed him in the right-hand pocket of her own jacket which was made from polyethylene terephthalate and the pocket itself was lined with rayon. Now, now, she said, as she stroked the curve of his back with her thumb, her four fingers shielding his head which rested against his knees, it is very bad that she is not here to meet us once again when we get off the bus from school. Where the hell could she be? What the hell could she be doing? Oh, she just sits in that room writing about her goddamn mother, as if people had never had a mother who wanted to kill them before they were born in the history of the world; and the stupid father named Mr. Potter who couldn't even read, and the fucking stupid little island on which she was born, full of stupid people whom history would be happy to forget but she has to keep reminding everybody about that place and those people and no one cares and she can't stand it. And where is she? She is in that little room off the kitchen, and from that room she can see the kitchen and she is making us whatever we all want to eat and none of us want the same thing and how she manages to keep writing that shit . . . make her stop, make her stop before I kill her and it was so much better when she would only knit us stockings that were too big before they were washed and then were too small after they were washed and they just gathered dust in the wash basket because she couldn't bear to throw them out, after all the time she had spent knitting them and the hats never kept us warm, they fell into our eyes when we were skiing and I almost killed myself coming down that black diamond wearing the stupid hat she had stayed up making for me as a present; and it is the stupid writing, it is the stupid writing, it is the stupid writing that's keeping her from being on time to meet the school bus that was driven by Mr. Strange, Ralph is his name too and that is not a name with a distinguished lineage, and a man, you know, who should be locked up in a jail in a cell that is buried underground, could come and pick us up and take us to his house and murder us or violate us sexually and we would never be seen again or heard of again, not even be mentioned on the nightly news, vanished from the face of the earth like a species from a geological era that isn't even yet detected—what is she doing, what is she doing, what the hell is she doing? She is sitting there in that room at the big desk that Donald made for her and she is thinking, thinking of a sentence and the way to end it: my mother would kill me if she got the chance, I would kill my mother if I had the courage, and as if such a thing were possible, she lives in that world of the room with the desk and the kitchen just beyond and she leaves us here all alone for a man to murder us, for tourists from Germany to stare at us, for all the other children and their mothers to see that she doesn't love us, she only loves the world that she carries around in her head, a torrent of lies, all in her head, we are nothing to her, nothing, nothing, only those words in her head, and now look, the night is coming, the ink-black night is going to swallow us up and we will never be found, for we will be lost in the night, the night itself, as if it were the ink-black sea.

•

Where is she, where is she . . . ? Then, oh just then Mrs. Sweet appeared in the old car, the old gray Kuniklos, the old car Mrs. Sweet fondly called Mr. McGregor, for she so loved to personalize everything, as if everything in the whole world were made solely for her; and when she saw her two children she blew up like a soufflé and actually right in her mind right then was the menu for dinner: crab soufflé, a salad of a mixture of newly sprouted leaves, the seeds had been purchased from Renee Shepherd and they had come in a packet that had been designed by the Shakers, a now extinct sect of devout people, with a French vinaigrette, ice cream if the children wanted it, from the store, not ice cream she had made herself— that she only did in the summer; she was very proud of them, and why? She couldn't say, not now, not then . . . But the children were glad to see her or so she thought then. His sister had released the young Heracles from her pocket the minute she caught sight of the old gray Kuniklos as it crested the hill just in front of the Gatlin house; the young Heracles had unfolded himself from that eternal fetal fold and now he looked fresh like a flower just opening, or like a flower just opening as seen in a time-lapse film. Mrs. Sweet gathered up her dear children in her arms and drew them close to her with eyes closed as if they were a fragrant bouquet of *Lilium nepalense* just then picked, but really though she hustled them into the back of the old car and there was mold growing on the floor, the roof of the car had a leak in it, the door on the driver's side did not close properly, letting in rain or snow as the case may be. In third gear, she turned onto Silk Road, crossed the Walloomsac River at the covered bridge, swiftly rounding the curves on Matteson Road, making a left on Harlan and then home to the house in which Shirley Jackson had once lived. But that journey home then, what of it? What of it now? For a forest stands between the covered bridge and Shirley Jackson's house and just as they approached it the beautiful Persephone passed her tongue over her lips and just as they crossed the boundary that separated town and village she then burst into song, not a song with everyday notes, not a song heard on the radio, and then again, it was not even a real song, it was a series of pitched sounds, each of them different, and they came in rows of twelve or maybe thirteen or fourteen, but twelve seemed more plausible, or so Mrs. Sweet thought, but she only thought this, she didn't know with certainty then or now, as she writes this; and those rows of notes that were the same and then were not, for the orderings were not expected, thought Mrs. Sweet, and that was when she didn't want to put a large man's athletic sock in the opening of the beautiful Persephone's mouth, the orderings were random, thought Mrs. Sweet, and that was when she wanted to throw the beautiful Persephone into an oblivion, an oblivion that was solely the heavens, a place where she would be held until Mrs. Sweet could bear her very presence again. And the beautiful Persephone sang as if she were backed by an entire orchestra, a lavish one, as if she were in a great hall and an audience with no defining physical characteristics, no broad noses, no fine and yellow hair, an indifferent complexion, removed from historical events, was listening to her. But to the ears of the other occupants of the old Kuniklos, a car that was made in Germany but bore a Greek name, how annoying to hear the contents of the Delia's catalog in that way, how annoying to hear the contents of the Wet Seal catalog in that way, how annoying to hear the contents of the beautiful Persephone's desires in that way. She sang on, though singing, that act, so associated often with the feeling of being transported out of your current state of mind into another realm, a realm of something other than your real self, was not what the beautiful Persephone did; she sang and the singing itself was beautiful and she sang of the tweed coat whose hem fell just below the knee and the tweed coat that was cut in the style of a seaman in the British navy and of the dress that was made from barrels of oil that had been wrought into fabric that looked like gossamer and a dress of surreal beauty was fashioned from it, and she sang of the skirt that had wide pleats and was short and of the skirt that had narrow pleats and was long and of the boots that were thick-soled and of the boots that came up to the knee and of the boots that could not even be considered worth wearing by the beautiful Persephone or her friend the flame-haired Lamb who lived on Mechanic Street, or her friend who lived on the ramparts of a mountain in North Adams, Massachusetts, or her many other friends who lived in the summer along with her at Eisner Camp, in Great Barrington, Massachusetts. Her voice at the same twelve pitch and then in a row that might be familiar and then unexpectedly not, or so it seemed to poor, benighted Mrs. Sweet's ears, for Mrs. Sweet only knew of Anglican hymns and then the Mighty Sparrow and then Motown and then disco and then the young Heracles loved Jay-Z, how cruel to make you love one thing twelve times and then change to something else and make you love that and then change to something else and make you love that too and then make the thing you loved new and not tell you and then you love that too and then change to something you had forgotten and make you love that too and then change to something you know and loved then and love now and make you think you don't know it at all. How cruel! So thought Mrs. Sweet. So thought Mrs. Sweet, as she drove her children to their home, the house that was the house Shirley Jackson had lived in. And as Mrs. Sweet approached the house, that beautiful house, painted white with Doric columns built in something called a Victorian style, she thought that the twelve pitches arranged in a row and then repeated over and over again and then changed unexpectedly might be as beautiful as trees arranged in rows of five diagonally placed and evenly spaced and therefore called a quincunx, and this repetition, this design, is so deeply restful to the spirit, and Mrs. Sweet could testify to this, for she once saw this very thing in the woodland part of a garden in Tuscany.

The twelve rows of notes, each the same, each varying slightly one from the other, so it seemed to Mrs. Sweet's untutored and Third World–attuned ears, came to a sharp end, the beautiful Persephone shut her mouth, and Mrs. Sweet brought the gray car, which was named by the carmaker to honor a rodent much loved by children and hated by anyone with an unfenced vegetable garden, to an abrupt stop! The children said, "Jesus Christ, Mom" and "Oh fuck, Mom," as their bodies lurched forward and then were restrained by the seatbelts which Mrs. Sweet always insisted they wear, and this unexpected flirtation with disaster would have been a delight and a thrill were it to take place on a ride in an amusement park, but not in the driveway of their own home sweet home.

Oh then, oh then, but only to see it now: for the young Heracles rushed into the house, through the doors, into the world of a cavalcade of imaginary figures, Ninja Turtles, Ninja Bats, Ninja Boys who wore exquisitely styled capes in colors too vivid to be found in the known world and they fought and triumphed over creatures from the world to come, creatures from the world that was, and they were to be seen on television or VHS tapes, not at all on *Where in the World Is Carmen Sandiego?*; and the beautiful Persephone rushed into the house to instant message Meredith and Samantha and Joan and Iona and Jenny and another girl with whom she shared special memories of Eisner Camp in Great Barrington, Massachusetts, and another girl whose father looked at vaginas all day because he was a gynecologist, and another girl whose parents tended a bed and breakfast in North Adams, Massachusetts, and another girl she had not yet met in person and never would meet in reality, and this absence of reality saddened Mrs. Sweet, for reality made up Now and Then, and Now and Then were without difference! Now and Then were not the same and yet Now and Then: for here was Mrs. Sweet and now she had two children and Mr. Sweet was her husband, the father of her two children, that was her Now and that was her Then, all being separate, and the separated formed a straight line that would now converge then, so thought Mrs. Sweet, as she followed her children into the depths of the house in which Shirley Jackson used to live, and it is true that the young Heracles and the beautiful Persephone had never heard of that woman who had lived in that house with the great big Doric columns, Victorian and Greek revival architecture. And what now? For Mrs. Sweet was entering the house, and just before she did that she paused on the threshold and then she stood very still: at her feet lay her life, it lay buried deep in an infernal-darkness, wine-hued or not, and it was guarded by a flock of her winged fears: "Not long after I had been made to copy Books One and Two of *Paradise Lost* as a punishment for misbehaving in class, I went to visit my godmother, Mrs. DeNully, a woman so large that she was unable to walk from the sofa to the chair without support, and if she had no support she would not have been able to do it at all. When she was not asleep, she stayed in the room that contained the sofa and some chairs, Morris chairs, and many bolts of cloth in every imaginable weave, or every weave available to the haberdashers in the British West Indies. These bolts of cloth came to her from mills in England and they were very good quality and not everybody could afford them: the woman who cleaned the DeNullys' house got from them as a Christmas present three yards of cloth. There were dotted Swiss and Irish linen and beautiful seersucker and embroidered cotton and silk faille and all sorts of things that would make a beautiful dress even more so in the room with Mrs. DeNully. Mrs. DeNully was married to Mr. DeNully and he worked as a manager at Mendes Dockyard, and it belonged to the family by that name and they sold all things to do with a ship and all things to do with a house. He had come from Scotland without money and without family to Antigua when he was a very young man, sixteen or so, and not long after that he met and married Mrs. DeNully. She was then the illegitimate daughter of a rich man; her mother was descended from slaves and her father was descended from masters and she looked more like the masters and less like the slaves. Her mother and father were never married. Her father was married to a woman with whom he had a daughter, his only legitimate child. This daughter and Mrs. DeNully looked very much alike, but they hated each other and the hatred was so firmly established that no one even knew really when it started or what was the cause of it. This daughter married a man named Pistana and I don't know now where he came from but sometimes people said Portugal. But Mrs. Pistana was in the haberdashery business also, and though the two sisters never spoke to each other they often referred customers to one another if the customers were looking for a kind of fabric that the one of them did not have in stock. In truth, they carried the same kinds of cloth, the one did not carry for sale something that the other did not. The kinds of cloth they sold came in one same shipment of dry goods, in the same ship, that left the same port from England. But it is Mrs. De-Nully I am thinking of now, and when I mention her sister Mrs. Pistana and her husband Mr. Pistana, who sold pots and pans and cups and plates in the other half of the establishment that he and his wife owned, it is only to make Mrs. DeNully alive to me now as she was then.

"Mrs. DeNully had four children, three boys and one girl, but the girl died a long time ago, how long ago I did not know then, and the time the girl was alive was never mentioned at all. It was around the time I was go-ing to the Moravian school and so I must have been around five years of age or six years of age, when I began to see her every day. I went to her house to have my lunch, for her house was right next to the Moravian church and my school was built on the grounds of the church in the eighteenth century by Moravian missionaries from somewhere in Germany. It was all right to approach her house for my lunch, for then the two dogs that were the pets of one her sons were locked up. They were not guard dogs, they were pets, and to show that they were pets and not just mere animals they were fed food that people ate, not spoiled food or food scraped from the bottom of the pan or other food that no one wanted to eat. But then, in the afternoons, after school when I was expected to stop by and say a thank you and good-bye to my godmother, that would be Mrs. De-Nully, the dogs often were no longer locked up; the son, whose pets they were, would have returned home from his school and the dogs were then let out. From a distance, they could see me leaving my school and crossing the field and the old graveyard and the lawn of the Moravian minister's house and then, when I was not too far from the old cistern, they would run toward me and pounce on me and throw me to the ground and then stand over me panting. Their names were Lion and Rover. Lion was the color of a lion, a lion I had seen in a book; Rover was just a dog and it was he who would always put one of his front paws on my small trembling body and then rest his own bodily weight on it, then lift himself up and hold the other front paw aloft and as he did this he breathed heavy and fast. I then wanted to cry but not with tears from my eyes or a sound from my mouth,

I wanted to cry from my stomach, because all my feeling was in my stomach but I didn't know how to do this. Then the owner of the dogs would appear, magically, for I had not seen him at all, and he would look down on me and rub his dogs' heads and call to them by their names and feed them hard-boiled duck eggs as he walked away from me."

Seeing then now, that small child that she was, vulnerable like the young bean vines that she should remember to water, for she was starting her own vegetables from seeds this year, and if they were not taken care of, if they were not looked after, they would shrivel and die, as that small child shriveled and died only to become Mrs. Sweet's Now, and to live on forever inside her. Unreachable, is that child; inconsolable and unreachable, but there she was, Mrs. Sweet, little pleats of fat girdling her not-so-youthful-anymore waist and no amount of running the four miles around the Park McCullough house with Meg could help that; her upper arms were the size of the pig's tenderloin on sale at the Price Chopper, her legs were still enviable, if only you could see them beneath those dreadful overalls purchased from the Gap and Smith and Hawken, and when Mr. Sweet was saying his eternally last goodbye to her, he looked at her in her overalls and said, I will be interested to see the man or woman who would find you desirable; and at that, Mrs. Sweet wept once more again and again also; and at the knees, the pants permanently blackened from her kneeling on the ground, weeding or planting something with a hard-to-pronounce Latin name. There then was Mr. Sweet intruding into Mrs. Sweet's line of accounting for her own being, there in her mind's eye, and she crossed the threshold into the mudroom of the Shirley Jackson house, opening the door to the kitchen, walking across the pinewood floors, standing in front of the stove, washing some dishes at the sink, preparing the ingredients for a crab soufflé, while the voice of the beautiful Persephone was cascading down the stairs, for she was in her own bedroom, and in that very tone that she had sung on the way home she sang: why are we having French food, is this a French restaurant, this is not a French restaurant, I want to go to McDonald's; and then she sang on: you think you are with us, you think we think that you are with us, but we know that you are really inside your own head and only what's there is real to you and you live in that little room with the big desk and we mean nothing to you, only your childhood with all its pain, as if no one had ever suffered in childhood, as if only your mother had ever been cruel to her own child before; and then, right then, all her words swelled into the high whine of a powerful body of water falling down through rocks that have been cast asunder by a violent eruption from the earth's belt itself or somewhere nearby and now were resting precariously with the uninterrupted flow of water passing over and around and below it and all this was situated at an altitude feeble with oxygen, and the girl's voice was painful to the ears, the pattern of rows and rows of notes, repeated in order and the order repeated again, was so painful to the ears. But Mrs. Sweet proceeded to make a crab soufflé, following the recipe of a woman who lived in Cambridge, Massachusetts, but who was a specialist in French food that no French woman Mrs. Sweet ever met was interested at all in cooking. However, and this was one of the ways Mrs. Sweet had of making See Then Now neutral, robbed of its power to cast powerful feelings and shadows over the people gathered at the dinner table, or the basketball tournament organized for the children who can't play very well, or the argument that will eventually lead to the divorce courts and the realm of child support, or the injustice of child support for someone who had children but had never given serious consideration of how to buy bread for them, or the ways in which to make a violation mute and dismiss its consequences! However, and even more contemptible: whatever! Mrs. Sweet continued on her way, deliberately ignoring the serpentine contempt in which her very being was wrapped and strangled as she entered that world of Mom and Mommy and Mother and so on; and she made dinner and set the table herself, for the children refused to do it, they were busy with making a replica of Hadrian's Villa for Latin class, replicating the viaducts that brought water from the Tiber to the Roman home, and household objects, useful or simply decorative, that were to be found in that Then known as Roman civilization: and all this homework was to be presided over by a teacher named Mr. McClellan.

And at dinner: the soufflé had not enough salt in it, too much salt in it, not enough crab in it, too much crab in it, the crab was stale, that was certain, frozen, for how can there be fresh crab in a village in a state that is landlocked? There are no land-dwelling crabs here. The salad was limp, Mrs. Sweet had poured the vinaigrette over the tender leaves a long time before it was eaten.

141

The beautiful Persephone made an island out of her salad as it sat on her plate, the collapsed portion of soufflé was a beach where a vicious pirate of Elizabethan times ruled or where vicious people who came from Haarlem sunned themselves because winter in Holland can sometimes be vicious. The world is vicious, thought Mrs. Sweet to herself, as she sat with her husband and two children at the dinner table. Mr. Sweet said in a loud voice, as if he were on a stage and addressing an audience: all the tulips your mother planted last autumn were eaten by the deer, a deer with six antlers, a clever old deer with good and malicious taste; the deer came and ate them all, just as they were about to bloom, just as they had reached that point in budding before bursting into bloom, the deer came and ate them, each bud a delicious juicy morsel of something that was perhaps holy, perhaps not, but they ate them, chowed down on them, devoured them, leaving your poor mother nothing but tall stalks of green, where there should have been, glistening with dew, "Queen of the Night," "Holland Queen," "Black Parrot," the little *clusiana* "Cynthia," "Lady Jane," the *humilis* "Alba Coerulea," *turkestanica, kolpakowskiana, linifolia,* Kaufmanniana hybrids and Greigii; where there should have been single, early blooms of "Purple Prince," "White Marvel," and "Christmas Orange"; where there should have been double, early blooms of "Mondial," "Monsella," and "Monte Carlo"; where there should have been lily-flowering blooms of "Mariette," "Marilyn," and "Mona Lisa"; where there should have been Mrs. John T. Scheepers, especially Mrs. John T. Scheepers, for that is your mother's favorite tulip of all tulips;

where there should have been all these treasures that she had looked forward to all winter, sitting in the bathtub and drinking ginger ale and eating oranges way into the middle of the night, dreaming of tulips and dreaming of ways to be alive that only enrage me (Mr. Sweet), and she does it solely to enrage me, for I (Mr. Sweet) want her dead, the beautiful Persephone and I want her dead, the beautiful Persephone and I would ask the young Heracles to kill her but he loves her so much, but now, at this moment, this now, what happiness, for the deer ate her tulips just as they were all about to open in a glorious bloom. And the two children burst into applause and clapped their hands and raised their glasses of milk in the air, even spilling some of the liquid onto their plates, the food now looked like something to be described by people interested in the obscure and unusual, and then they burst into a chorus of: who got her turban, deer got her turban, who got her turban, deer got her turban, who got her turban, deer ate her turban, call and response, response and call, and it all reached a crescendo that broke to the ground, twelve discordant notes, none of them meant to be together. Mommy, Mommy, Mommy! Mom! Mrs. Sweet's children sat across from her, their breath was her breath, and it smelled of all the sweet things she had given them, and their names were the beautiful Persephone and the young Heracles, not Rover and Lion, and in any case they had never heard of and so could not have eaten the eggs of ducks.

Gathering her children to her bosom, Mrs. Sweet soothed them with kisses, reminding them that they loved her then, not only just then, but that then when they were babies and couldn't fall asleep without her milk-yielding breasts in their mouths, of that Then when they couldn't cross the road and she had to show them how, of that Then when the young Heracles could only be lulled into a stupor by being taken to a place where men operated huge machinery and the machines made noises that were so loud you could not hear yourself think and the men were in the process of realizing some marvel of engineering; of that Then when she took them to see the Continental Divide and a receding glacier in the state of Montana and unexpectedly found a species of clematis, *columbiana*, in bloom right outside the kitchen of the motel where they were staying, and inside their breakfast was being cooked and this was just before she learned that the path to a lake named to commemorate a woman who would have been a pain to have as a friend was closed because some German tourist had been knocked down to the ground by a grizzly bear the day before, the bear's real purpose was to consume a baby elk that had been swimming in the lake with its mother. Herding her children to their rooms upstairs in the Shirley Jackson house, Shirley Jackson being a woman who had been long dead by the time Mrs. Sweet was living in that house and a woman Mrs. Sweet would never know, but her being nevertheless was all too present even as she was unknown to Mrs. Sweet as she went about the everyday: Mrs. Sweet tossed them into their beds without incident, for by that time putting the children to bed was such an ordeal for dear Mrs. Sweet, so full of bargains made around the packed lunch: would Mrs. Sweet put extra Oreos so the beautiful Persephone could share with Joree, whose parents did not allow her to have sugary things; would Mrs. Sweet allow the young Heracles to have a playdate with Gregory, whose parents were devout Christians attached to some branch and sect that Mrs. Sweet could not understand. And after all she allowed the young Heracles to go to Gregory's house for a visit though at the same time she prayed or wished, prayers and wishes then being interchangeable and indistinguishable, that no harm would come to him, and no harm ever came to him when he visited Gregory's house. All the same, Mrs. Sweet was so relieved to hear that Gregory was soon moving to Florida. But just before he could let go of her—because he sensed she was longing to go back to that much-hated room, the room just off the kitchen, the room in which she would commune with the vast world that began in 1492, the room in which lay her mother and her dead brother and her other brothers and all the other people whom she sought out even as they had turned their backs on her, that room, that room: burn it down, cried her children, burn it with her in it, cried Mr. Sweet, but Mrs. Sweet knew of no other way to be and in any case did not know that her existence and her way of being caused so much as a stir in others—but just before he could let go of her, just before he drifted off to sleep, a state of being he fought mightily against, for the young Heracles sought to dominate, not to be dominated, he said to his mother, Mom, Mom, oh Mom! Tell me again of the Dean and Mrs. Hess and he was referring to those tales of two deep-sea-dwelling creatures, a man and a woman who were married to each other and who did this without having gills and without having lungs. The Dean had grown up in a place called Oxnard, California, where for two or three or four generations his family made hats for all kinds of people and the people wore the hats to every kind of event: to church, to work in mines where they extracted from the seams of the earth all sorts of things that are featured prominently in the periodic table, to drink beer in a bar, to marry each other, to attend a funeral, a baptism, a bat mitzvah, a bar mitzvah, to assassinate someone, to pay a visit to someone recovering from a serious illness in the hospital, to go to the bank to repay a loan in installments, to attend ceremonies of customs that originated in not well-understood parts of the known world, Africa just for example; but the hats that were made by the Dean's family were now integral to these customs and the people who wore the hats had no interest in the people who made them at all. Mrs. Hess had grown up in a place called Massachusetts and for generations her family made furniture from the trunks of maple trees and oak trees and ash trees and butternut trees and pine trees of various species and all kinds of people ate their dinners and had conversations and rendered judgments of a legal kind or of an everyday conversational kind; that was the world of Mrs. Hess. They now congregate within the pages of a book and their ups and downs, all taking place deep in the watery bowels of earth and even deeper than that, in places where the earth's substance was not water at all but only something like it—liquid; and when Mrs. Sweet read that to the young Heracles, he would say, what does that mean, not water but only something like it, come on Mom, come on Mom, is it water or is it not water and Mrs. Sweet would proceed as if she had not been interrupted and the young Heracles would recede as if he had not interrupted. But in any case, the adventures of the Dean and Mrs. Hess, these two people, who without precedent inhabited and were familiar with the watery depths of the earth as if it were a surface and they knew depths beyond this depth, this so thrilled the young Heracles.

The Dean and Mrs. Hess possessed neither lungs nor gills, for they did not live in water or on dry land, for they were not yet of this earth as we now know it, but they did see the earth grow dense and large and larger still; they did see an inner core become covered with an outer core and then that become covered over by a mantle. "Well, look at that," said Mrs. Hess to the Dean, just as inner core disappeared beneath mantle. At that, the Dean adjusted his glasses. "This is exhausting," he said and Mrs. Hess said, "You think so, just wait till we have children." The Dean wanted to say, "What's that?" but he knew that Mrs. Hess hated just then any unusual amount of irony and she might interpret his attempt at humor as inappropriate. He said nothing. He looked at his wife, her hair a beautiful rust, her eyes the color of a fire as it is reflected in the glass eyes of the two cats that decorated the andirons in the hearth of a fireplace in New England in mid-November; he looked at his wife as she spun around and around first in one direction, then in another in an effort to make herself at one with the earth's own turning; she failed and sank to her own center. And the Dean said, "What's that!" and then for a while, he turned molten and silent. And then he boiled up, not in resentment and anger but in laughter and much clapping with approval at his own happiness. He loved Mrs. Hess. He loved her so much! He bombarded her with kisses which she sensibly ignored but took note of nevertheless. "Is it time for dinner?" asked the Dean and Mrs. Hess replied firmly, "Not yet!" and time moved on in the way it always would, always will, then and now intertwined, losing uniqueness, difference, distinction, subject only to laws of human consciousness. "Mom, Mom, what's happening? Where's the time when the Dean eats the plate full of hot horse chestnuts, fresh from being roasted in the immortal fire, you know, the fire that is burning forever at the center of the earth, the one that is waiting to turn us back into the thing from which we came, that thing called the universe? Where is that? Can you get to that chapter, please? I want to hear about the millions of years of rain. Can you skip to that, please Mom, please Mom?" The young Heracles loved the sweet mellifluous tone of Mrs. Sweet's voice as she read to him the story of creation, the story of how he Now was Then, the very story, the nature of any story, the story being the definition of chaos, of the unstable, of the uncertain, of the pause that holds the possibility of nothingness, empty. And Mrs. Sweet continued in a very steady voice, for the personality of the reassuring mother came readily and easily to her: she said, while speaking for Mrs. Hess, "It rained a kind of water that was so complicated with various elements and each of them separately or combined, it would not matter, would be inhospitable to the life of the mosquito who was a vector of the most virulent form of malaria

and it rained for one hundred million years." The young
Heracles, said, "Oh Mom, oh Mom, can we go to Africa?" But Mrs. Sweet, still speaking as Mrs. Hess said,
"Not yet is there an Africa, not yet is there an Africa,"
saying it twice, for that would make it really so and it
was really so then and it is really so now. "Well enough
of this, young man," said Mrs. Sweet, for she could see
the to and fro of traveling to Africa undifferentiated
from Now and Then, just a landmass emerging from
billions of years of the earth's relentless restlessness, the
earth indifferent to a unique individual consciousness as
it might manifest itself in Mrs. Sweet, the young Heracles, or anyone else; and she brought the bedsheets and
down comforter, mixed up as they were, sheets and
comforter, to his chin, and folded them around his body
as if he were in a shroud but he was only going to sleep
and would wake up the next morning, not going to
sleep forever. He lay in the bottom half of his bunk bed
that Mrs. Sweet had purchased from Crate & Barrel, and
Mr. Sweet had objected to the cost of it; the top half was
left for the young Heracles' friends, Tad and Ted and
Tim and Tom and Tut, and such were their names and
they were not afraid to fall out of a bed so high up from
the floor, or so they said, and the young Heracles did
not believe them. And just before she left him, just
before she showed him the moon and said goodnight,
Mrs. Sweet said, "Tomorrow is another day and what
will you do then?" for she was familiar with seeing now,
in any case dreaming. Mrs. Sweet closed tightly the book
that contained the adventures of the Dean and Mrs. Hess
but the Dean and Mrs. Hess were not concerned at all,

149

they continued as always, as before and after and as they do now: the Dean's glasses slipped down from the thin banister that was his nose for a moment, a moment of millions of years in the realms of the batholiths and into formations of thickened fluids that solidified into granite, rocks becoming stilled through cooling. "Oh yes, oh yes!" said the Dean and Mrs. Hess to each other, as they traversed the deep realm, before there was any surface which was habitable, and they were creating a surface which could be made habitable, but they were not at all interested in that then.

The time passed. But did time pass? Yes, it did and the Dean grew hungry and said to Mrs. Hess, "Dinner?" and she answered, "Not yet!" for it would be many ages before such a thing was possible, dinner: the purchasing of meat and vegetables from the supermarket, cooking them, setting the table, sitting down to eat them while going over the events of a day, the way we live now. The way we live now! Yes, the way we live now: the tawdriness of it, the small-mindedness in it, the importance of the self, the self degraded not properly valued, the self of no use, of no comfort to any individual. The way we live now! The Dean sighed and lay down, and Mrs. Hess, thinking this a secret from him, continued to turn this way, flip that way, in imitation of the earth's magnetic field, but how could such a thing be unknown to this god of geomancy? Iron-nickel alloy, peridotite, gabbro, granite—all known to him by hand and heart. "Well, all right," he said to her and the eras and periods and epochs, too, flew by in his mind's eye: Cambrian, Devonian, Permian, the 'cenes, and there were many of those, the 'cenes. The green plaid of the duvet, under which lay the young Heracles, moved up and down in a constant perfect rhythm, the beat of his heart it was, but then he shifted violently and his hand swung out into the air and came to rest on the top of his covering, there his hand lay isolated like a part of a landmass, submerging or emerging, neither one nor the other. But he was dreaming of flowers, of fields upon fields of wheat in flower, and then flour, and flowering trees that would bear fruit, and then some that would bear nothing edible, and his whole night was like that: dreams of flowers and flours and fruits and flowers that were beautiful for their own sake.

8

When I was a child, said Mrs. Sweet to herself, speaking to herself in her mind's eye, her lips that could be seen not moving at all, her eyes fixed on the stitches that the needles made as they slipped from one to the next under her guidance, for she had taught herself the ways of knitting, slipping the knitted stitch off the needle and then retrieving it by twisting it in the opposite direction, making it raised as if it were a pearl and this stitch was called a "purl," and even so Mrs. Sweet understood that her method of doing this would meet with the disapproval of any Olympian authority; and Mrs. Sweet was making a baby's blanket, following the instructions of the authorities that would frown upon her, producing a Vandyke check pattern, a series of stitch-and-purls, and at that time she was not expecting a child but: When I was a child, she said, I thought the world was first still and then all of creation had come into being solely for me and that I was born on the Seventh Day. I did think that, really and truly so, until I was about nine years of age and then something happened and what was that?

Before I was nine, before that, something happened. I do see now that there was much turbulence and upheaval in my life, but all this had to do with my own creative narration, my own individual creation: I was not allowed to cry when I was being scolded for some transgression or the other, and I had so many, for I was always being scolded, and I was so ashamed of my imperfections, though if I had been left to myself I would have been perfect: there was not a thing about me that I found wanting, not my thoughts, not my physical appearance, not my mother, not anything she did or did not do. All of my sadness and all of my longing and all of myself was accepted by me. But I seemed unable to do anything that pleased anyone and that included me, my own self, though at the time I did not know that myself constituted such a thing as an existence. I couldn't please the people I knew and so I couldn't please myself. A whole life is distilled from some event that occurred before you are three years of age or after three years of age but not past your sixth year; a whole life can span six thousand years and each year consists of 365 days excepting for a leap year, and it would remain so: that a whole life is made up of some small event, fleeting, something so small, deeply buried within itself, a catastrophe, not easily detectable to you or to the careful observer, but visible enough to a lover or a roommate or the person living next door who does not wish you well, the event, which in fact becomes your greatest flaw, occurs when you are most powerless to thwart its occurrence, when you are most unable to make its malignancy benign, when you are most unable to shrug it off, as if it were nothing more than a leaf falling off a tree in October, a change of seasons, a phenomenon that is quite apparent in parts of the earth's atmosphere, yes, yes, that is what makes up a whole life, the small event that cannot be seen by you, but can be seen by random people, and that small event makes you vulnerable to the deep and casual desires of these people, random or select, you can never know, really know. All this said Mrs. Sweet to herself as she resided in her mind's eye, and she knitted a garment, this time it was a sweater made up in a pattern to be worn by men who lived on an island adrift in the northern part of the Atlantic Ocean and this island was formed there in that period of time called the Lower Carboniferous and these men who lived on this island wore this garment to sea. The Aran sweater it was that she knitted, the stitches were knit two purl two and knit one purl two, or purl two knit one drop one, or drop two and then pick up one or pick up nothing at all, and in that way Mrs. Sweet continued: I was not allowed to cry; so many times I wanted to cry, so many times, but when I did, I was scolded so harshly, I was told that my tears were a sign that I was proud like the fallen hero of a paradise that was lost, that I was Lucifer or something like him, and when I was seven years of age my punishment for misbehaving in school was to copy by longhand Books One and Two of *Paradise Lost* by John Milton; and at that time I lived without artificial light, that would be light provided by electricity, I lived then in a little house with my mother and her husband, a man who was my father by association and that association made him more important to me than my father through biology; and I copied those chapters, Book One and Book Two, and I identified with Lucifer, who did not cry, but it was not something I knew in the way I knew I preferred to be hot than to be cold. But I did cry: I cried when my mother took me with her to the St. John's Public Library when I could not yet read, and she read many books all to herself while I sat on her lap and looked up at her lips which never moved but her whole being, her body, was transformed, for she did not remain the same.

But life, real life, the way a life unfurls, is never as you have imagined it: so said Mrs. Sweet to herself, as she sat packing up a trunk of clothes for the young Heracles who was then going off to golf camp with his friend, the equally young Will Atlas, and Mrs. Sweet was going over in her mind the scene of Mr. Sweet saying to her, well, I know you are trying very hard but I love someone else and I will not give her up, for she makes me feel like my true self, my real self, who I really am, I am in love with a woman who originates from a far different climate and culture than the one you are from and she is very sweet in nature, quite like me, and she plays all the Brahms everything with four hands even though she only has two just like everybody else, and she is young and beautiful and can bear children who are beautiful and sweet in nature like me and they will never need Adderall; Mrs. Sweet then, that is, while Mr. Sweet was saying all these words that made up sentences and made sense and yet didn't, for that little man dressed in corduroy trousers and a wool plaid jacket that was in the style of a gentleman hunter in rural England and saying those words that broke her sweet heart, she could not have had anything to do with such a person, but all the same that man in those clothes was her husband, Mr. Sweet, and then, right then, she understood all the little scenes that had come before: that January, when she suffered most from the lack of heat from the weakened sun, Mr. Sweet took ballroom-dancing lessons and she wanted to join him in this exciting activity, and when she suggested it he exploded in a rage that would be worthy of a suggestion that he drop an atomic bomb on an island nation in the Pacific Ocean but then calmed himself and said to her, politely with a smile, well no, you can't do that because Danny and Susan, and then for Mrs. Sweet all the words that followed in that sentence vanished, for there was the beautiful Persephone and she needed all sorts of things to be sent to her while she was boarding at Eisner Camp or St. Mark's School or just in summer residence somewhere, and then there were the bills to be paid for the upkeep of the house, which was the Shirley Jackson house, or so it was called by all the people who lived in that village, which lay on both banks of the river called Paran.

Oh Now, oh Then, said Mrs. Sweet out loud, but it didn't matter, it was as if she said it to herself, for no one could ever understand her agony, ever, ever understand, her suffering, her pain, no words could express it, nothing in existence could convey or express her existence just then, now or ever, her husband's voice, her husband had been enfolded in an entity called Mr. Sweet.

I am dying, she said to herself but that was silence; I am dying when I am with you, said Mr. Sweet to Mrs. Sweet, I am dying and that is why I hate you, for I am dying and I can't be myself, my true self, I am dying and you will die when I say this, but I am dying, I am dying, I am dying. Oh I see, said Mrs. Sweet out loud but even she couldn't hear herself, and all that she saw, then and now, was silent!

But she then could see the young Heracles sitting on a couch in the children's room, watching Michael Jordan and Scottie Pippen and Dennis Rodman defeat Karl Malone and John Stockton, and Michael Jordan, who then had a very bad cold and each time he made a score he almost fell down but his fellow teammate Scottie Pippen was always there to hold him up, and the young Heracles, who worshipped Michael Jordan, held his opponents in high disregard and said they were lame, and Mrs. Sweet knitted and purled all the while, listening to her son whoop and shout and moan and cry out in agony at the very idea that his beloved Michael Jordan's team would lose, but then they won and the young Heracles said to his mother, hey Mom, I know you are going to say this is just like Homer, this is just like the *Iliad*, and there is Agamemnon and there is Achilles coming up to save everything, admit it Mom, you're gonna say it's just like in Homer in that funny little voice of yours as if you're on the radio, 'cause you talk like someone on the radio, your voice is official but you're just my mom and you're so ridiculous I don't know what I'm going to do with you, you are so embarrassing; and Mrs. Sweet knitted away, for she was right then making the entire orchestra that would perform Mr. Sweet's suite of nocturnes, but much to her surprise, when this chore was completed the performers were all missing one of the arms they needed to play their instruments. So inevitable are the series of events seen over your shoulder as you glance back from the series of events that stand before you, and in your own mind you can see the series of events that are to come, that are arrayed before you, and they appear as if they are in the rearview mirror but only in reverse, only as if the rearview mirror could make visible the thing that has not happened yet, for perhaps Time, said Mrs. Sweet to herself as she knitted away those garments with one sleeve missing, was a father, not a mother, and Mrs. Sweet had no father, that is, she had not been authored, she had been created by a very malicious woman. Oh Mom, oh Mom, can't you see, said the young boy to his mother, and he was jumping up and down, running this way and that through the assembled crowds of shy Myrmidons, Ninja Turtles, Power Rangers, Super Mario, Batman, various figurines from Star Wars, various stuffed animals, some resembling the domesticated, some resembling wild ones who were now extinct; and they all lay before him and also they all lay before him in his memory so fresh, so fresh and so clean, so, so sorry, Mrs. Jackson, that they still inhabited his Now; and the boy, the young Heracles, was now involved in the sadness of worrying about Ken Griffey, whose father had been a legend of baseball lore, or so the young Heracles told his mother, and the young Heracles loved the young Griffey and so was involved in his fate, which might not be so full of glory as was his Michael Jordan and Scottie Pippen and

Dennis Rodman; but just then, as he was sitting in his chair in the children's room, his father Mr. Sweet said to him, I must tell you something and Mr. Sweet said, I don't love your mother anymore, I love another woman who comes from somewhere else, another woman with whom I have been taking ballroom-dancing lessons and we talk about Mozart, for she plays the pianoforte excellently and she could be the next extraordinary piano genius of the century, the century is long because centuries are long, though in your life you might, ha ha ha, find them not as long as I have found them, but I love her and nothing can change that and I don't love your mother, you know, we were always so incompatible, for she did emerge from a boat whose main cargo was bananas, and she is strange and should live in the attic of a house that burns down, though I don't want her to be in it when that happens, but if she was in it when the house burned down, I wouldn't be surprised, she is that kind of person. And on hearing all this, oh nooooo, was a long howl of pain that came up and out of the bowels, through the darkness of the mouth of the young Heracles, and he furled and unfurled again and again like the petals of a flower as it comes into bloom and then fades rapidly so did the young Heracles, who had only been sitting in his chair in the children's room, watching on television the young ballplayer Ken Griffey in the process of being or never being the great baseball player all the baseball world thought he would be.

And Mrs. Sweet now broke in two as if she were made of something to be found in the Pennsylvania formation but she was not made from that, she only knew of that; and she wept and wept over the broken body of her son, who now lay on the couch, the television was on but Ken Griffey was not on Mrs. Sweet's mind, Mr. Sweet never cared for baseball except he liked Willie Mays and could say things about Willie Mays and that was all so great, seeing greatness in a child's book; and Mrs. Sweet broke in two continuously, kept breaking over and over again, never into many pieces, just the same two, her heart, her head, and especially her heart, and shortly afterward the wiring in her heart became erratic and had to be ablated. But then, right then, Mr. Sweet elaborated to the young Heracles on all his disenchantment with the young boy's mother: she snores horribly; she smells of the past, for she is growing old and so am I, said Mr. Sweet, but young women like me and I do not like old women, said Mr. Sweet, your mother is old; she has come to like Wittgenstein but she does not understand him; she likes *Erwartung* but she does not understand what she reads, she is very naïve, she is very primitive, she is very amusing, she is wonderful when you are trying to be brave, but when you are with her and you face your limitations, she's a joke, she's an embarrassment, she's not my type, we are incompatible. But Dad, but Dad, said the young Heracles, what am I gonna do? and now he crumpled into the shape of a piece of paper on which the wrong thing had been written and it had been thrown into the waste receptacle never to be thought of again, and Mrs. Sweet gathered up her sweet son and wrapped him in a blanket she had made and in that one garment there was no error and she wrapped him up in it and put him in the bottom part of his bunk bed, a bed made of ash and purchased from Crate & Barrel.

•

In the corner of that room in which the young Heracles heard the indictment against his sacred mother, he loved her so, he thought her ridiculous, her obsession with plants and the flowers and fruits that they bear; her wanting to wear jodhpurs made of denim, the uniform of workmen in some faraway country, to parents' night at his school so all the other parents could see that she wasn't at all like them; her love of cooking food that took a long time to prepare: duck with plum sauce, that took days before it was ready to be eaten; the other mothers didn't know that she could sing all the words to "Stan" and that she loved Dr. Dre; she once went off to China and spent weeks there collecting the seeds of plants she could grow in her garden; that time she told a man who was taking his family on a shopping outing to Manchester and he took her parking spot before she had a chance to position her car properly, maybe your dick will fall off, and the man, who had never been spoken to like that before in front of his treasured family, became enraged, so much so that it filled him with shame and he almost collapsed from it but he soon recovered and did not yield the parking spot and he proceeded to the Ralph Lauren outlet and was never seen again by the young Heracles; and Mom is so ridiculous and she is so ridiculous and Mom is so ridiculous, and he thought of the time when she had taught him to make her a martini so he could bring it to her at half past five in the afternoon while she was in the garden doing something that nobody in the rest of the family cared about, and there was this day when

Mr. Sweet came into the house and said to the young Heracles, have you seen my beautiful wife? and the young Heracles answered, no but if you're looking for Mom, she is in the garden, and Mom, who loved the garden as if it were a person or something like that, so thought the young Heracles, and none of the other mothers were like that, none of them thought the garden was like a person and had an individual need and that it called for attention and care and could enrich your inner life, so thought the young Heracles, none of my friends' mothers were like Mom and it is so embarrassing, Mom is so embarrassing, if she wasn't my own mom I would have gone out and found a mom who wasn't like her at all, a mom who was just like the other moms, for Mom is so embarrassing. And just outside the room in which corner lay the shy Myrmidons and the Ninja Turtles and the Power Rangers and Darth Vader and Luke Skywalker, though never at all Princess Leia, and Batman though never at all Robin, just outside that room was the tree house that Rob had built with the wood Mr. Sweet had ordered to measure from Greenberg's lumber store, and Rob had nailed the wood into the evergreens that had been planted in the yard just outside the Shirley Jackson house, and beneath the tree house was the sandbox: the tree house was only a platform with the overgrown branches of the evergreens casting a veil of green tears around it and it harbored insects that fed on its secretions, and the children, that would be the beautiful Persephone and the young Heracles, hated it, and so they stayed beneath it, where it formed a canopy for the sandbox; in the sandbox was a bench and table all in one, like the ones provided at a public beach or a state park for the random passerby, for sometimes the children would pretend they were such people, the random passerby at a beach or a state park, for they lived in the mountains, for Mr. and Mrs. Sweet had never in their married life, never in their life as the parents of two healthy children, participated in that family tradition, that transforming and celebrated event called the family vacation, for Mr. Sweet was afraid of spaces of every kind, be they open or enclosed. And in that sandbox was a miniature John Deere tractor that was of no real use, only it made the young Heracles, while sitting in its seat, believe that he was a farmer reaping an imaginary crop of no particular kind in an imaginary field, or preparing the imaginary field for the imaginary planting season to come and just generally being an imaginary man in command of a powerful piece of machinery and just generally imagining himself as a person who would be strange to his parents, Mr. and Mrs. Sweet, for they had purchased the toy farm machinery and they had also purchased the toy backhoe made of strong plastic and the miniature buckets and the miniature spades and forks and wheelbarrows, all toy-sized, all useless, all having nothing to do with the real and true people they wanted the beautiful Persephone and the young Heracles to become.

Oh now, knit and purl, knit and purl, ten stitches that way, twenty stitches the other way, drop some number of them now, pick another number of them up later and form a pattern that will then be shaped into a wearable garment, or a covering for a bed: for what is she doing now? She has taken up knitting? At least it's not costly: gardening is costly; the terrace and wall cost forty thousand dollars; a replica of a cottage at Yaddo wouldn't cost that much and poor Mr. Sweet could use such a cottage, for he composed his compositions in a room above the garage and from there he could hear the spinning of the washing machine and then the sharp whir of the clothes dryer, and doors banging shut, not in anger but thoughtlessness, and the screams of the children from pain or pleasure, and that bitch singing, "Where Did Our Love Go," and that word "love" shouldn't be allowed to cross her lips, for she knows nothing about it, that sweet secret of feeling, that precious thing, that moment in which your heart meets the heart that complements its own true self, that colliding of feelings between you and another that emanate from deep within you, deep within your heart, your stomach, your bowels, your loins, just between you and another, so unexpected, so powerful that it causes the furnace of the house in which I have been living with an ignorant bitch to explode, and then love soothes with nocturnes for pianos played by four hands, festivals, and lessons in ballroom dancing too. And all those thoughts flowed out from Mr. Sweet, unknown to his wife, as she sat in that unknowingness, that space invisible to the naked eye, and tried to sort out how she came to be herself, and unraveling various parts of the garment that had been her own life: the hem of this garment had become undone, it dragged on the floor and it had become dirty and from time to time it made her trip over her own self and stumble and she fell down and scraped her knees and bruised her forehead and her elbows too, the hem needs to be mended, thought poor Mrs. Sweet, the hem needs to be made more secure, for the elbows and knees and forehead, these were just the parts that were visible, all the parts of her that the unraveling garment caused to be bruised could not be seen, not even by her, only felt sometimes when the salt of her tears dried in their shallow crevices.

Oh Mom, oh Mom, Mrs. Sweet heard those words, though to the person from whose being they came they were not words at all, they were life itself, and that person was the beautiful Persephone and that person was the young Heracles, and in those words, oh Mom, oh Mom, she could see and imagine herself as their mother and their protector and their navigator in a world in which the circumference was known: the children were calling out to their mother but Mrs. Sweet so liked to live in her garment: the shroud of her past, her childhood, her life before that, her life as it was interred in all the people she was descended and ascended from; her own life right then, right now, so sweet to her, each moment of her everyday existence so full of satisfaction: her two children who were to be woken up from sleep early in the morning to be dressed in clothes she had warmed up in the dryer, for they hated to put on cold clothes, and fed a breakfast of waffles, the batter made the night before and placed in the refrigerator, and on top of the waffles she poured maple syrup she had purchased from a man who lived on a farm on the road to Shaftsbury, a village that lay to the west of Lake Paran, and before pouring it on the waffles she warmed it up in the microwave oven; she made a fire in the fireplace and they sat before it, a screen placed between them and the flames themselves to protect the children from the hot flying embers; she bundled them into the car, a gray car of one make or another, not too expensive, a product of some country, not this one, drove them to the bus stop where they boarded the yellow school bus, entrusting them to a bus driver who might be in a bad mood or not, it all depended on the behavior of the other children who had boarded on the many stops before. And after she had seen the school bus disappear down Monument Avenue and pass the church in whose graveyard lay buried Robert Lee Frost and some of his children, she then got into the car and drove slowly back the way she had come, pass the Gatlin house, turning onto Silk Road, crossing the covered bridge on Silk Road, driving onto Matteson Road, turning onto Harlan and then coming to her own house, the house in which Shirley Jackson once lived. Inside now, it was as if the children, her own children, did not exist, only herself as a child did exist, and she now entered the temple, the sacred heart of her own life: See, Now, Then, and so it went on and on, these visitations, a holy journey into her past, around and around that room in which she sat and examined her life as it had been, as it was, and as it would be, for it was all the same, always just as it ever was and always just as it ever would be:

"To be abandoned is the worst humiliation, the only true humiliation, and that is why death is so unforgivable, for life has abandoned you and you are left all alone, by yourself, apart from everything, so that you are not even nothing, all that you used to subjugate, that person or thing or event, is lost to you in death, and no memorial, no in memoriam, no monument erected to you can erase the fact that in death you are powerless to act, you are no longer in Then and Now, you are no longer anything and only exist at the will of others and only exist if they desire you to exist, for your existence might be of use to them, and then when it is not you are abandoned again, put aside for something else, and that would be Now again, for Now is ongoing and never ceases, Now is unrelenting, impervious to everything known, and even unknown, impervious to all that can be grasped and held down firmly to all that can be grasped and held down firmly—and to be abandoned is the true, true nature of humiliation and to be in a state of humiliation is death and to be dead is to be humiliated, for then you cannot even know your situation and pity yourself. Now, Now, Now, which represents living itself, which represents life itself, defeats you and makes rubbish of you, the discarded, something caught in the wind on an empty street, aimless, aimless. Now, Now, and Now again: for that instant that is full of everything that makes up your true life but is always just out of reach, first seeming only an arm's length away but forever out of reach, and the effort makes you tired but you can see it just out of reach and you try to catch it again but it is just out of reach, always it is out of reach, and you try again and again but the moments pile on top of each other and they are always out of reach, and then death itself is a moment that is never out of your reach but death itself makes you unable to make the effort of reaching"—so said and did say

Mrs. Sweet to herself, as she entered her house, now empty of the children, now the fire before which they had eaten their breakfast was only embers, now beckoned her room, the infernal room in which she brought alive all that had made her, that room off the kitchen that had in it the desk Donald had made for her, and she knitted a garment for herself.

•

Oh Mom, oh Mom, cried the young Heracles, so broken he was then, lying on the couch where before the events that led to him saying, oh Mom, oh Mom, he had been watching: basketball, tennis, golf. Oh Mom, oh Mom, he cried and he crumpled as if he had actually been defeated by all his labors, all the tasks that had been set before him, one after the other: the Nemean Lion, the Lernaean Hydra, the Cerynitian Hind, the Erymanthian Boar, the Augean Stables, the Stymphalian Birds, the Cretan Bull, the Mares that belonged to Diomedes, Hippolyte's Belt, Geryon's Cattle, Hesperides' Apples, capturing Cerberus, when it is well known that in every telling of these tales he triumphs again and again, but not so now, and his mother wept and wept to see him so crumpled up, like rubbish, a piece of paper waiting for a light breeze to dispatch it to its destiny; and their tears, his own and his mother's, remained separate, for she wept from a sense of failure, she had failed to keep him from knowing the bitterness of a weak and jealous father, she had given him a father who knew nothing of it, who knew not at all how to love a son, how to treasure a son and keep him whole, keep him one complete being, whole and intact, each seam of himself tight, impermeable, and all meant to give him a sense of his own inevitability to become a whole man, to see him become a father of fathers, gentle and kind, full of love and generous in this, and not become a tyrant, a traitor, mean in body and in soul; but she had not found for her young Heracles a father who could love him so much that he would rather be extinguished and not ever be known to human consciousness, a father who would rather be dead than to cause him to crumple on the sofa just when he was in the midst of watching Sunday-afternoon football on TV. Oh Mom, oh Mom, and he folded up as if he were a croissant, that was something he loved and Mrs. Sweet used to make them for him, even though they could be found in the frozen-food department of the supermarket made by Sara Lee, and she made the children a pound cake, using the recipe from *The Art of Fine Baking* by Paula Peck, even though a pound cake could be found right next to the croissant manufactured by that same entity, Sara Lee. And he folded up and so did his mother, the dear Mrs. Sweet, for she was dear when loving her children, even if she could from time to time be misguided, or irrelevant, or hopeless, and she couldn't bear to see them suffer, and it was all this that made her create the room off the kitchen into which she would enter and disinter her past, what used to be her Now and had naturally become her Then, as in Then I was, Then I did, Then I became, and as she folded and crumpled into a heap of pain and hurt alongside the young Heracles, who was then folded up into the shape of part of his breakfast and the representatives of his imagination inside and outside the room, and by that time her own mother was dead and she was glad that such a person who had been so instrumental in her own existence was no longer alive, such a person who could and would have rejoiced at this significant moment of Mrs. Sweet's abandonment, was not alive, was dead, and death has no Then and Now.

•

And Mr. Sweet said, I love your mother, I loved your mother, I will always love your mother, she is so dear to me, the dear Mrs. Sweet, but she is so awful, did you hear the way she talked to the waiters, she is so objectionable, I would never tell you this because I really couldn't, in our house we celebrated Christmas and Easter and we were never rude to people who waited on us and your mother would be of the people who waited on us but she your mother was so interesting, when I first knew of her, she was interested in the arrangement of the firmament and I bought her a telescope for her birthday and she loved insects, butterflies especially, and I gave her a net to catch them for I knew of Nabokov and she didn't know of Nabokov and it was such a pleasure to see her delight in all that I could show her, she really rewarded my efforts but then she grew into a monster and one day I noticed that she was rude to waiters and I could have been rude to waiters but I knew that such a thing was wrong; but one day she went to Alldays & Onions to get special capers and she saw the waitress speaking kindly to a man, an ugly man, and the waitress said to that ugly man, hello handsome, what can I get for you today? and after the transaction your mother said to the waitress, how can you speak so to such an ugly man, and the waitress said, that was my husband. And your mother returned to me and she was filled with a description of fields of pink flowers that were shaped like fists and it was to see this, the fields of pink flowers like fists, that made her take that route to the Alldays & Onions, and it was there she insulted the waitress and her husband and that was the final straw, it was then I wanted to be with someone who wouldn't instinctively be unkind to people who waited on me and my mother and father and my brother and his familiar, and your mother was someone who couldn't make such a distinction. I wished she minced words, I wish she would bite off her tongue, I wish she would simply become dead. Oh young Heracles, Oh young Heracles, where are you? Are you under the blanket of my despair that is your mother, that truly abominable woman, your mother Mrs. Sweet?

Oh now, oh now, that was Mrs. Sweet making a tale of the events that had been Now, which always soon became Then, as she tried with resounding success to keep the young Heracles from approaching and so entering the gates of Austen Riggs or some such institution, or approaching the gates and then occupying the rooms and hallways for people who had been abandoned by their mothers and fathers and brothers and sisters and aunts and uncles and cousins and radiating outward as far as is possible and then going downward as far as is possible, and it was from such a situation that his mother sought to save him, as he sat on the couch, folded into the shape of something delicious to eat at breakfast, and his father told him that he no longer loved his mother, and that his mother was a lovely person but he no longer loved her, he loved someone else; and the young Heracles had no other way to understand this except in this way: the beautiful Persephone would ridicule Mrs. Sweet's love of flowers because Mrs. Sweet would buy plants in quantities that exceeded the space in the garden in which she could place them and the young and beautiful girl would observe her mother's dilemma and pretend that she was a purchaser of plants ordering them on the telephone: "Hello, do you have Madonna detroittii disgustiphilum? And how much is that? Ninety-nine cents per one hundred? Can I have a million of those please?" and this would cause the whole family, that being Mr. and Mrs. Sweet, the beautiful Persephone and the young Heracles, all to explode in laughter at Mrs. Sweet's extravagance, Mrs. Sweet's foolishness, and in any case Mrs. Sweet believed that to provide amusement and laughter to her family was not unlike providing dinner. But then there was the ridicule at dinner and that was Mom's roast, like something at a gathering of comedians who said mean but true things about each other and the event was impersonal and profitable in all sorts of ways, but at the Sweets' dinner table Mrs. Sweet could see the laughter that her vulnerabilities provided but she was not made happy to hear her faults and flaws presented with fondness: the plants that cost so little individually but then when presented in a bundle were expensive and her family could reveal that she did not really understand the true cost of the material of her daily life; and this was so devastating to Mrs. Sweet, for her history, her very being, her current existence, was deeply involved and could be used as an illustration of the true cost of daily life, not a precise daily life, but an approximation of one. But there at the dinner table, with the beautiful Persephone and the young Heracles and Mr. Sweet himself, was Mom's roast, as if they were at some event in which Jonathan Winters would make an appearance and say funny, memorable things and there in attendance would be other people like that too, but this was Mrs. Sweet's dinner and the other diners were her daughter and her son and her husband, and her husband no longer loved her, her husband hated her, and this was not unusual in the fragile structure, made up of bones and muscle and blood and a soul too, known as a husband, and this was not unusual in the fragile structure made up of a woman, a man, two children or more, known as Family Life.

Oh Now, oh now, said Mrs. Sweet to herself, for she was then looking into an abyss, but that would be literature; for she was now looking into the shallow depths, a structural depression, but that would be geology; and at the bottom of this metaphor or just a true representation lay her life, the remains of it, the facts of it, the substance of it, the summation of it, the finality of it, the good-bye for now and see you later maybe of it, the end in the beginning of it, and Mrs. Sweet wept, for she had loved her life so much; and this was a surprise to her, that she had loved her life so much: the life with Mr. Sweet and his foul breath after a good night's sleep, his slight stature, the hair on his beautifully pear-shaped head disappearing in a calculated way, as if it was being harvested for a purpose unbeknownst to human imagination; her dead mother lying in a coffin and being looked at by all the people she had made feel small and all those people were so glad to have outlived her and Mrs. Sweet was among them. And seeing then: the portraits of them, Mr. and Mrs. Sweet, the day after they were married, which had been taken by Francesca, and on the day they received the canceled check they had paid Francesca with for the expenses incurred for the film and other things, a sum of fourteen dollars it was, that very day Francesca had jumped off a building, and Mrs. Sweet made herself forget that the building was situated on a street in the narrow landmass of the lower part of Manhattan; Mr. Sweet's fear of growing trees, with the cycle of budding and leafing out and becoming themselves for a season and then their growth dimming and eventually coming to a temporary pause, growing dormant and resting and then budding forth again, and Mrs. Sweet found this process a joy, its inevitability a mystery, unexpected, unimaginable even, and she would order even more plants then, but Mr. Sweet said to her not once but again and again, I only love dead trees, and she hadn't paid attention that he was saying that he didn't love her, that he didn't love her, that he didn't love her, she only thought that he loved trees when they were dead, for it is so that when you love someone you make them say the things that are pleasing to you, the things that will make you love them more, and you never hear what they are saying right then and now, right now and then; but there was Helen and her paintings of night with its quarter moon, and a lone woman looking up at a dimly lit sky, and then Helen and Mrs. Sweet going for a run on the still-elevated West Side Highway and running and running and then while doing so they could see men having sex with each other and they had never understood how men had sex with each other until then, until then, and Helen said, wow! but she said, wow! about everything, so Mrs. Sweet said to herself, Then and even Now!, that is how Helen spoke; yes, that was Helen and is Helen now and also then.

Listen to this right now, Mr. Sweet was saying, I love you but I don't love you in the way I love someone so superior to even myself, someone I shouldn't be allowed to even speak to she is so wonderful and outside any realm I have ever known, and Mrs. Sweet heard all these words but couldn't understand them really and could only see Mr. Sweet as he would one day be covered with small worms crawling and crawling though going only from his head to his toes and no further than that and then his whole body was like lacework, beautiful and useless, waiting to be turned into something, the bodice of a dress or the top border of curtains, something seen in passing and in the end annoying: listen, Mr. Sweet was saying, and now Mrs. Sweet turned into not stone but a mound of mud, and sorrow became her middle name if she possessed one but she did not then and not now, and she sank into her ancient landscape and that would be memory and that would be her mother and that landscape had a horizon and she longed again and again to see the end of it, to see the horizon and stand on it and see the thing it held or the nothing within it: my mother was very beautiful and I was so ashamed of this, I was so ashamed of my mother's beauty.

"I used to be ashamed of the very day on which I was born, for it was the twenty-fifth of May, not the twenty-fourth, and on that day, the twenty-fourth of May, there was a fete on the grounds of the Moravian church, it was called a May Fair, and girls, beautiful girls whose features even then made no permanent impression, for they were subjects and their very being, their existence, depended on this event, the twenty-fourth of May; and the fete had a main event, which was the may-pole and the dancing around it of those girls of unstable beauty and it was such an honor at that time, then and now, as the case may be, and they danced holding ribbons of red or white or blue, attached to the pole, and they went toward the pole and away from the pole and toward each other and away from each other and made a pattern around the pole so that the pole was covered with the blue and white and red ribbons; and then when I didn't know I could love the clothes I was wearing, when I didn't know that the way I appeared to other people was something to think about, that time then, when my mother had a friend who was a stevedore and he lived down at Points and my mother and I lived on Dickenson Bay Street in a house with two rooms, just the two of us, and we used to go and visit her friend the stevedore; he was a short man and thick and wide, like a figure I might see in an illustrated children's book: a stevedore, and he lived in a house from which I could see the loco full of the product that had come from freshly harvested sugarcane going from the factory to the ships waiting to receive it and take it to England, which was far away, way, way beyond the horizon; and then my mother and the stevedore would be swallowed into his house, the house in which the stevedore lived, a darkness, and I was never allowed inside it; and when my mother and the stevedore disappeared into that house and left me alone, I played with my shadow, I imagined my shadow was a girl, and we played with each other and read to each other books we had written, and sometimes we were two girls in England, and we were in a garden with flowers but only flowers and that was enough, for flowers are the furniture of a garden wherever the garden may be, and the stevedore's garden had only portulaca, though then I was told, how I can't tell now, it was a rose that spread around. Then in the stevedore's yard, where I was left alone while my mother disappeared with him into his house that was so dark inside that my mother never allowed me to enter, I would dance around on the spots where the portulaca, or so I call it now, grew and those spots were far apart and between that and watching the loco pass by and seeing the Points School where one day I would be a student and seeing the silhouette of Rat Island in the distance, I kept myself, my true self, though I did not know her then, together and all in one piece and so when my mother emerged from the stevedore's house and took my hand and we walked back together to the house in which we lived and she carried a sack of brown sugar, the kind of brown sugar that was just granulated from molasses, the kind of sugar that was to be used every day, for on Sundays we used white sugar, but in any case my mother never allowed me to eat anything with sugar of any kind, except on special occasions. But what was a special occasion?

"Oh, and she was so beautiful, I was so ashamed to be seen with her; she had very long hair and she wore it rolled up and pinned to her head as if it were a kind of treasure and then I came to know that it was the way women in Guadeloupe and Martinique styled their hair and she also spoke patois and wore clothes that the other mothers didn't wear, tight skirts with a split in the back starting at the hem and ending a third of the way up; and men looked at her and then stopped and talked to her and she never looked at them but then would stop and talk to them and walk on and everybody knew, she was my mother and I knew she was my mother and loved her and all of that: the stevedore, her hair, her clothes, her smell after I bathed her back in the galvanized bathtub full of water that she had perfumed with bush, her red lips, her cruelty to me, the way she left me aside when something new came up, something I didn't know could exist: one day she fell in love with a man and they had children, three boys eventually, but before the first one was born, I understood, no not understood, for even now I don't understand what Then was Now, even now I see then as translucent, as if it is all taking place on a pane of glass and sliding that way and just when it is about to disappear into nothing the pane of glass tilts this way, back into seeing Now and Then there as it all is just before it goes into another Then and Now, another Then and Now and seeing all of it only in a blink."

•

"Things change," Mr. Sweet was saying to Mrs. Sweet, "Things change!" But that was the harsh version, for he was in a state of rage, his voice was like a Wilkinson razor blade, newly emerged from that ironmonger's factory, his arms jabbed at her but stopped short of making contact with the inconsolable mass of flesh, heaving with sorrow and then resting from that. "Things change, Sweetie, things change." And he twitched his hips and shook his head vigorously, dancing to a music that was heard only by him, or so Mrs. Sweet said to herself on seeing him then, and then he began to hum out loud parts of *The Rite of Spring, The Sea, The Cat, The Spider's Web, The Rat, The Dog, The Child's Bed*, and after he was done with that he said to his wife, now shorn of her former dignity, Mrs. Sweet, and she was wearing a lovely brown dress made by Lilith, I never loved you, you know, I never loved you, not because you were unlovable, though really you are, no one could love you, not even me who knew nothing about love then but now I do and I see that I never loved you, for you are like walking into barbed wire in the dark, you are like an invitation to a tea party in an ant nest, you are like, you are like, I can't any longer right now think of what you are like, so said Mr. Sweet to Mrs. Sweet, and just then, right then, she was so beside herself with grief and she wept and her tears watered the *Primula capitata*, which she had planted under the giant white pine tree and so her tears were most welcome by that delicate plant, native as it is to the moist regions of the Himalayas. And she wept and wept and Mr. Sweet spoke to her as she was bent over the parched primroses, themselves wilting and prostrate on the ground, suffering from the harsh conditions under which they were forcibly being cultivated, in the crotch of the roots of an evergreen native to Canada though they came from the Himalayan region of the world; and Mrs. Sweet wept and wept and wept some more, for Mr. Sweet said then to her, you are just crying because you know the children and I will never forgive or forget the terrible things you have said and done, and that made her die a death in which she was still alive, not dead at all, but still alive, and yet dead, for he showed her life as she had been living in it, the moment when the beautiful Persephone had to be put to bed at dusk but she resisted it always, for she wanted to be with her parents, they did things that were mysterious to her, and she would delay that moment when she would be placed in her crib, for she had not yet outgrown it, and the thickly woven cotton blanket would be drawn up and carefully arranged under her chin, for her arms were folded up into her body like a bird if you were baking it as a delicious dish to be served for dinner. Mrs. Sweet died and died and in this way she lived for a long time, dying over and over again, never coming to a rest, a state of not then, not to come, not to have been, only now, only die and die and die, and Mrs. Sweet died, she did die and never again wore the denim jodhpurs that had been given to her by her friend Rebecca who had seen them being worn by municipal workers in Japan when she was on a visit there.

Each day has twenty-four hours, each week has seven of those days, each year has fifty-two weeks, and it is so, and the age of the earth is made up of more than four billion years, of those years and weeks and days and hours, then, now and then again, forcibly enclosed in it, and it was and is and will be so, Mrs. Sweet said to herself over and over again, as if it were a song that been carried on the wind and she had heard it and taken it to heart, a song heard while walking along the banks of the Battenkill River for twenty-eight miles, and she stood still then, seeing in her mind's eye the winding course the river would take ending with it emptying itself into the Hudson River some distance away from that place where the sea's tides influence the river.

All that is to come will change the way right now is seen; right now is so certain, right now is forever; what is to come will make, distort, and even erase right now; right now will be replaced by another right now: and right now is all there is and all there is over and over again and no welling up of the fluids in the individual stomach, a universal metaphor for the unstableness of the whole human enterprise as it is experienced by the person making breakfast for the litter of domesticated mammals before her or him, and the boy and girl with Game Boy or Super Mario in hand, as the case may be, no matter how it is heard, no matter how it is felt, and it is such a disappointment, right now, for right now is always so incomplete, or so we feel, and that is a blessing, for it transforms then into what will come, all that will come, even though all that will come must contain right now and the unfathomable longing for the then, that time to come after the earth was Precambrian, Hadean, Proterozoic, Paleozoic, Cambrian, Ordovician, Silurian,

Devonian, Cretaceous, and Lower this and Lower that and then Upper that too, and then Cenozoic and rifting and volcanic, that time to come after the earth was itself, that time to come was the time that had been before, for beyond the earth's boundaries, was all that had made it, was all that it had been and is and the future was the past and the past, which is then, it is always then, could be found in the periodic table and Mrs. Sweet looked up and saw that pinned to the doors of the pantry was a map illustrating the principles of that thing itself, the periodic table, the beautiful Persephone showed an interest in chemistry and her mother had purchased it and placed it there and then Mrs. Sweet looked out the window, through the panes of glass that separated and shielded her from all that lay outside the Shirley Jackson house, the house in which she lived with her children and her husband and she could see a landscape so different from the one in which she was formed: that paradise of persistent sunshine and pleasant weather, a paradise so complete it immediately rendered itself as hell; outside now there was spring and in it, on the banks of the river Paran and stretching out onto the flanks of the Taconic and the Green Mountain ranges, were large trees, some of them evergreen, some of them deciduous and right then in bud.

9 780374 534363